About the Author

Rosanna Moss was born in Bristol and currently lives in Peterborough. She enjoys reading, writing and trying to learn Spanish. As well as this, she loves to spend time with her four grandchildren. *The Testament of Abigail Williams* is her second book.

The Testament of Abigail Williams

With many thanks
Rosanna Moss xx

Rosanna Moss

The Testament of Abigail Williams

Vanguard Press

A CIP catalogue record for this title is
available from the British Library.

ISBN 978 1 83794 082 0

Vanguard Press is an imprint of
Pegasus Elliot Mackenzie Publishers Ltd.
www.pegasuspublishers.com

First Published in 2024

Vanguard Press
Sheraton House Castle Park
Cambridge England

Printed & Bound in Great Britain

For my grandchildren, Livy, Charlie, Sam and Jack, with my love, always.

Dedicated to those who lost their lives in the Salem Witch Crisis of 1692-1693

Special thanks to all family and friends who continue to support my dream. You know who you are! Thanks also to Pegasus Publishing for their guidance.

Prologue

Jane cracked the egg and let the white from it ooze into the warm water in the teardrop-shaped vase. This was what the whispering inside her head had told her to do. She discarded the yellow yolk and egg shell, throwing them a little distance away from the small group of girls made up of her sisters. Together, they watched as the egg white began to coalesce in the water. What message regarding their future would it give?

Suddenly, the mood was broken. Alice Samuel, the old woman who lived next door to the girls, could be heard shouting at them as she hurried across the field they were in, shaking her fist. She arrived at their little circle in a breathless state of anxiety.

"You silly girls!" she remonstrated. "You don't know what you'm playing with. You will be attracting the Devil," she continued, indicating the glass. She quickly bent over and tipped the contents onto the grass. The water drained into the soil, but the egg white lay on the ground as an amorphous, semisolid substance. "You shouldn't meddle with things you'm don't understand!"

The glass, although now empty of fluid, had a strange bright fog swirling around in it. The same fog that Jane had witnessed, for the first time, the previous night. She had taken a closer look and had heard a gentle whispering coming from within. Placing her ear to the rim, she had found herself being sucked in until the bright fog was all around her and then slowly the fog had parted to reveal a strange apparition – not quite man, yet not quite beast, with wolf-like yellow eyes – eyes that were full of mischief and malice – knowing eyes. She had slammed shut her eyelids. If she couldn't see it, it maybe couldn't see her. After a time, she had dared to open them and found that, somehow, she was back in her bed. All was fine. It had been a dream, and yet, she felt different... Full of a spiteful energy.

The girls, frightened by the old woman's actions, drew together in a huddle.

"You'm better run along home and say your prayers afore it be too late," the old woman ordered. "Go, pray hard, and I won't be telling anyone what I've seen here today."

The girls hurried away. All were scared. All, that is, except Jane. As they quickly covered the distance back to their home, Jane looked back to where they had held their gathering. The old woman was picking up the glass they had used for the oomancy. A deep rage began to erupt in Jane. *That old woman in the beastly black hat is going to pay for this*, thought Jane, her breathing becoming both faster and shallower.

Alice Samuel looked back towards the fleeing girls, as though she could feel Jane's rage washing over her. She bent to pick up the vase. It did, after all, belong to her. She had noticed it was missing the night before and remembered that Jane had paid her a visit earlier that day, delivering some eggs which had been gathered from the Throckmorton hens. Jane must have seen the vase and been enticed by it. It wasn't the first time someone had been led into temptation by the vase. The reason the Samuels owned it in the first place was because an ancestor had stolen it during one of the crusades to Jerusalem in 1291.

Once back home, Jane did what the voice whispering inside her head told her to do. She went straight to the room of Anne, the family's servant woman, and searched under her bed. Jane found what the whispering voice wanted, hidden deep in a basket. It was a bottle of liquid. Anne also practised as a midwife and made her own potion, from a secret recipe handed down from wise woman to wise woman, which she gave to pregnant women to help with their contractions and other concerns. Jane pulled the stopper from the neck of the bottle and drank some of the potion. "*Careful, not too much,*" said the voice in her head. "*Only enough to make you do, say, and see strange things.*" Jane replaced the stopper and wiped her mouth with her sleeve. The liquid was thick and tasted sweet and minty. She put the bottle back where she had found it. "*Drink a little of this every day,*" whispered the voice. Jane then went to join her sisters. Soon, she collapsed and, on the face of it, became quite ill. Her body contorted into impossible positions and she appeared to be able to converse with invisible beings. The family found her actions alarming. All attempts to try to find out what was wrong with the girl drew a blank.

Finally, in between fits, Jane stated that she had been bewitched.

"Who would do such a thing?" asked her parents.

"Alice Samuel," replied Jane.

1693, Boston Harbour, Massachusetts, New England

A sea fret was curling in from across the Atlantic. It wrapped itself around the young lady who was standing on the wooden landing, waiting to board a ship which would carry her back to England. Her belongings had already been loaded onto the vessel and all that was left to do was to say goodbye to her uncle, the Reverend Samuel Parris, who had accompanied her to the harbour. She risked a glance at him. He too was shrouded in the sea fret and he looked cold with a bluish tinge to his skin.

"Well, Uncle, it is time I bid you farewell," she said.

Samuel Parris looked at his niece, Abigail Williams, and wished he had never given her a roof over her head. He wished, God help him, that she had perished along with her parents in the Native American massacre of settlers. Instead, she had been taken hostage, along with others, to be used as a bargaining tool by the Native Americans hoping to swap the settler hostages for their own captured warriors. She had been trouble from day one and a bad influence on his daughter, Betty. Abigail, although having been very quiet and reserved and free of her supposed afflictions these past few months, was, nevertheless, leaving behind her a trail of deaths and broken homes. The village of Salem would never be the same again. Was he being harsh in his judgement of Abigail, he questioned himself. He had no answer. Abigail had only been ten when she had come to live with him and his family. A mysterious little girl with a curious wooden doll to which she had an unhealthy attachment.

"Yes, Abigail, time to board ship," he replied, looking over her head at the vessel in question. "You must try very hard to make a good impression on your father's family," he continued. "I know you have never met them before, but they are keen to take you in and give you a home."

Abigail nodded and turned to board the ship. Once she was on board, Reverend Parris wasted no time in hanging around and vanished into the mist as though he had never been there. Abigail sighed. It was obvious to her that he was relieved to be passing her over to her relations.

Her uncle had contacted the Cromwells in Huntingdon, England, and pleaded with them to take over responsibility for her. Her father had been a distant relation to the Cromwells, and so they had agreed. They had sent the money for her passage as the Reverend Parris could not afford to send her back to England out of his savings. He hadn't been paid fully for his position as reverend to the village of Salem for a while now and the village committee had also stopped the allowance of £6 for his wood, despite this being part of the agreement between himself and the village committee at the time of his appointment. The parsonage where he and his family lived was now a very cold place as the wood stock at the back of the house had almost run out.

It was true that Abigail had never met her father's family and knew next to nothing about them. However, she could remember her mother recounting a tale to her about a young girl called Jane Throckmorton, an ancestor on her mother's side (Uncle Samuel was married to her mother's sister and so was related to Abigail by marriage) who had suffered strange fits and had accused the family living next door of bewitching her. It had been a common belief that Jane had stolen a vase from the Samuels, a vase which had its origins in the time of the Crusades and that the Samuels were punishing her for the theft. This had taken place about one hundred years ago in a village called Warboys in England. Eventually, the three people who were accused of witchcraft, Alice Samuel, her husband John and their daughter, Agnes, had all been hanged. It had been of particular interest to the Cromwells at that time, because Lady Cromwell had visited the Throckmorton family in an attempt to try to sort out the problem and had, herself, become very ill and, it was believed, been bewitched and had later died as a result. To Abigail, this story had been fascinating, and although it was not clear how the actions of Jane and her sisters, who also came to be afflicted with fits, had benefitted in any way from the execution of the Samuels, excepting that perhaps Jane was able to cover up her own misdeed of stealing the vase in the first place, Abigail was quick to understand how such torments could be put to good use in terms of gaining some sort of power over others.

When Abigail had first arrived in the village of Salem, she had become aware of underlying tensions amongst the villagers, particularly within her uncle's congregation. Constantly living in fear of being attacked by the Native American tribes, the residents of Salem, instead of being united through a common worry over their safety, were quietly at loggerheads with each other and a pervading atmosphere of envy and malicious gossip existed within the village boundary. Times were hard. They were mostly a God-fearing community, staunchly religious and extremely loyal to the word of God as they understood it, and so any accidents, disease, crop failure and such like was seen as a warning from God that he was not happy with their commitment to him, and as such, they were allowing the Devil to play amongst them. Consequently, the villagers asked questions of themselves. Who among them was not committed? Who, by laziness of faith or through a liaison with another power, was causing God's wrath? The community had been a cauldron of suspicions just waiting for the right spark to set the whole mixture bubbling over the top. It had been Abigail who had provided that spark.

One dark and dreary afternoon in January 1692, their chores for the day completed, Abigail and Betty had had time on their hands. Betty had asked if they could do an oomancy. The parsonage was quiet as both of Betty's parents were out and the servant slave, Tituba, brought to New England by Uncle Samuel from Barbados where he used to run his family's plantation, was on an errand. Abigail had unpacked one of her family's prized possessions which, along with Abigail, had survived the Native American attack. It was a clear glass vase, shaped like a teardrop. The very Venus Glass, so tradition within the Williams family went, that had first belonged to Alice Samuel and the same glass which Alice Samuel had regained on that fateful afternoon in November 1589. It had been part of the Samuels' personal effects which the Cromwells had taken possession of after Alice and her family had been executed. Somehow, over the successive years of inheritance, the glass, and its legend, had found its way into the hands of Abigail's father. However, the use of a Venus glass was seen as witchery and so this was why, it being a rare occasion that the parsonage was so quiet and the girls had a bit of time to themselves, that they were being secretive about their actions.

Abigail and Betty had settled themselves down in the kitchen lean-to of the parsonage. The glass had been filled with warm water and was put on the table next to an egg. For added atmosphere, the wooden doll had been fetched from underneath Abigail's bed and was placed on one of the chairs. The girls each sat on the other chairs. Abigail took the egg, cracked it over the rim of the Venus Glass and split the shell in half, carefully transferring the yolk from one half of the shell to the other whilst the egg white, or the clear albumen, stretched itself slowly down into the warm water in the glass. While they waited for the mixture to thicken into a pearly white shape, the girls speculated as to what they might see. The object of this oomancy, hopefully, was to foretell which man Betty might marry in the future. Betty had her eye on a boy who was the same age as herself and who worked on his family's farm. She saw him regularly at the Sunday morning sermon in the village meetinghouse. She loved his dimples and the way his blond hair flopped over one eye. She was very much hoping to see some shape which she could connect to him, form in the water in the glass.

Meanwhile, Tituba, having completed her errand, had returned to the parsonage. She was weary, for it had been a long busy morning of beating the rugs and sweeping. She was looking forward to a little relax while her master and mistress were out and she fervently hoped that she wouldn't have to entertain Betty, Abigail and their friends with tales of magic from her tribal childhood. She entered the lean-to and came to a dead standstill as her dark eyes grew very round and threatened to pop out of her head.

"The Lord protect us! What are you girls doing? You'll be letting in the Devil!" she exclaimed. Her long, black plaits performed a see-saw effect as she shook her head from side to side. "We must get this cleaned up afore the master sees it. He'll blame me for sure," she continued.

As she drew nearer to the table, she sucked in her breath in horror. The albumen had coalesced into a shape. Betty also drew away from the table, her action knocking over her chair. The shape was not at all what she was expecting to see. Instead of the much wished for likeness of her intended, the egg white resembled the shape of a coffin. Both Betty and Tituba clutched together in fear. Abigail's expression, however, carried an enigmatic smile. The same expression, noted Tituba, as was mirrored on the face of the wooden doll as it turned its head to look straight at her.

Chapter One

"Right, class, listen up," shouted Miss Jones above the din. She stood with her arms folded. A long chain with a whistle attached to it hung around her neck. She would give them ten seconds and then, if they didn't shut up and pay attention, she would use the whistle. It always gave results as the students couldn't stand its shrill noise. Her fingers began to twirl the whistle around. Catching the eye of Ricky Morris, she slowly began to raise the whistle to her lips. He quickly nudged his fellow pupils and pointed to the teacher. A sudden hush descended over the class.

"That's more like it!" exclaimed Miss Jones, letting the whistle fall back. "Now, this term we will be studying Arthur Miller's *The Crucible* as part of English Literature. As well as this, I have teamed us up with the Drama department as they want to stage a new version of *The Crucible*. So, I want all of you to write individual plays and I will choose some of the best to give to the Drama department for them to decide which one to stage."

Amid groans, Miss Jones distributed copies of *The Crucible* to each member of the class. When this task was completed, she told them to turn to the page which listed the cast of the characters.

"Oh!" exclaimed Ricky Morris. "It has a character by the name of Abigail Williams in it." He turned his head to look at where Abi Williams was sitting.

"Well done, Ricky!" retorted Abi. "That's common knowledge! Have you only just realised that?" She flicked her long golden hair back over her shoulder and continued studying her copy of the play.

Miss Jones nodded. "That's right, Ricky, it has. Now, *The Crucible* is in fact a true story. All the characters in this existed. However, Arthur Miller made Abigail Williams much older than she really was in his play. I think it was probably because he thought modern audiences would be able to understand better the reason why Abigail accused John's wife of witchcraft. Miller hinted that Abigail was in love with John and wanted his wife out of the way. In real life, Abigail was only around the age of ten or eleven and any hint of a romance between an eleven-year-old Abigail and a married man would seem, to modern audiences, distasteful."

"Paedo!" shouted another pupil.

"Exactly!" agreed Miss Jones. "In fact, there is a theory that Abigail and John didn't even know each other. Now, for homework, I want you to read through the play and to do some research on the real-life characters and the Salem Witch Trials. We are looking for a new approach to the play, so if you can jot down some ideas as well – this would be a good start."

The bell rang, which signalled the end of the lesson and also the end of the school day. Chairs were immediately pushed back and books shoved into backpacks, ready for the homeward journey.

"Now don't forget," yelled Miss Jones over the noise, "for homework, I want to see evidence of some ideas and knowledge of the Salem Witch Trials – look at the background to the Trials, what problems and worries did the villagers have at that time – did any of it have a bearing on what happened?" This last question was delivered to an empty classroom as all the pupils had gone. Miss Jones sighed and began to pack up her own bags. She knew it would be the usual pupils who would put in the effort. It was a shame, really, because she was very excited by the teaming up of the English and Drama departments.

Just outside the school gates, Abi Williams and her friend Michelle were waiting to catch the school bus home. Both girls had their skirts rolled up around their waists to give the impression that they were wearing miniskirts. They hated the normal length of the grey tartan pleated school skirt which reached down to just below the knee and made them feel frumpy. Several times during the school day they were asked to unroll the skirts by the teachers, but as soon as the teacher had gone, the skirts were duly rolled back up again.

Michelle pulled a bag of sweets from the pocket of her blazer and offered one to Abi. "I reckon Ricky Morris fancies you, Abi," she stated.

Abi chose a sweet from the bag and popped it into her mouth. "What on earth makes you think that?" she asked.

"Well, he's always looking round at you in class and never misses a chance to make some comment to you," explained Michelle.

"Does he? I hadn't noticed. I wouldn't go out with him, he's far too immature. I've got my eye on someone in the sixth form anyway."

"The sixth form! Abi, we're only in year ten! Someone in the sixth form is way too old," Michelle advised her friend. "Anyway," she continued, "that's news to me. Who is it?"

"David Smith," said Abi.

"Ugggh! You can't fancy him! He's horrible!" stated Michelle, wrinkling her nose in distaste.

"No, he isn't. He's got the most gorgeous eyes!" said Abi, defending her taste in boys.

"Does he even know you exist?" asked Michelle.

"Not yet," admitted Abi.

The truth was that, to date, neither girl had had a boyfriend. They were in that curious stage where boys their own age were a complete turn-off, yet they were too young to catch the eye of older boys, so they were reduced to merely dreaming of what could be.

The bus arrived and both girls hopped on, showing their passes to the driver. They made their way to the back of the bus and managed to get two seats together. They both lived in the pretty village of Warburton. Michelle had lived there all her life. Her father was the village rector and they lived in the vicarage. Abi and her family had only recently moved into the village. They had come from another local village, so she and Michelle had known each other since playgroup days, but Abi's dad had inherited Absalem Cottage from his grandmother so they had decided to move into it and sell their house. Abi loved the cottage. Her bedroom had a sloping roof and looked out over the large rambling back garden which eventually ran into a small wood. Just on the edge of the wood, but still surrounded by trees, there was a very large garden shed which had yet to be investigated. Abi had her eye on it and wanted to make it into a proper room with chairs and curtains. She suspected her younger brother, Ben, wanted to turn it into a den for him and his noisy mates. A squabble over it was on the horizon and Abi knew it would be settled by her parents either stating that neither of them could use it as it would be used for garden implements, such as the lawn mower, or that she and Ben would have to share it. Their younger sister, Nicola, had shown no interest in it at all. In fact, Nicola said it gave her the creeps and it reminded her of *The Blair Witch Project*, a film she had managed to watch, much to the annoyance of their parents, whilst on a sleepover at one of her friends.

The bus pulled in at the stop outside the village shop in Warburton and both girls got off. They walked a short distance together before splitting to go in the direction of their homes.

Abi walked along her tree-lined street to the cottage. There was a lane which ran down the side of the cottage to a back gate and Abi walked down this, unrolling her skirt to its proper length as she went. As she arrived at the little gate, which carried the nameplate *Absalem Cottage* and which only came up to her waist, she noticed someone was working in the garden. A hole was being dug and the person carrying out this task was stooped over in the hole, shovelling out earth and depositing it onto a slowly growing mound at the side. She watched for a little while and presently the person came up for air and hauled himself up out of the hole to sit on the edge. He was understandably sweating from effort as the day was very warm and he removed his shirt and threw it clear of the rubble. Abi caught her breath and her heart did a little flip. David Smith and his gorgeous eyes were slipping from her mind. This person right here in her garden was straight out of her dreams. Before opening the gate, Abi re-rolled her skirt to a dangerous length. The little gate gave its usual squeak as she entered the garden and the young man turned his attention to see who was arriving.

'Hello," said Abi, walking towards him with, she hoped, her best seductive walk. She caught her foot on a stone, wobbled and nearly teetered into the hole.

"Careful! Mind how you go. I'm afraid I'm not the neatest of workers," he apologised.

"I'm okay,' said Abi, her cheeks burning. "What are you doing anyway?"

"The owners want a garden pond, so I'm digging out a space for one," he explained.

"Oh. I didn't know they wanted a pond. Must have been a sudden decision, I suppose," answered Abi. The young man nodded. A short silence followed while Abi racked her brain for something else to say. "I'm Abi, by the way. I live here and it's my parents who are having this built," she continued, holding out her hand.

He wiped his hand on his jeans and shook her hand. "I'm Josh Harrison. Pleased to meet you." He grinned. Abi was interested to note that his grip was firm and dependable. The memory of David Smith was, by now, floating off to space like an escaped helium-filled balloon.

Abi's mum came out of the cottage carrying a tray with a glass of iced Coca-Cola on it, which she handed to Josh.

"Hello, sweetie," her mum acknowledged her. "How was your day?"

"Oh, you know, the usual," answered Abi. She was anxious to get out of the way in case her mother said something embarrassing in front of Josh. Also, she wanted to race up to her room and change out of her school uniform and into something more alluring. She picked up her school bag. "Gotta go. See you around, Josh," she said flippantly over her shoulder.

"Whatever length is your skirt, young lady!" exclaimed her mother in shocked tones. Abi gritted her teeth. Perhaps she wouldn't come back down after all. She would stay in her room and hope that the next time she saw Josh, he would have forgotten what her mother had just said. It was Friday today. Hopefully he would continue working tomorrow which meant that she would have the whole day to hang around.

That evening, after dinner, Abi was back up in her bedroom, lying sprawled on her bed. She considered Face Timing Michelle to tell her all about Josh, but decided against this. What, after all, was there to tell? No, she would leave it for the weekend and maybe tell Michelle on Monday.

Abi turned instead to her homework. She had to confess to herself that the idea of writing a play, which might be staged by the Drama department, filled her with enthusiasm. She determined to find out all that she could about the real-life characters in *The Crucible* in the hope that maybe she could offer a new perspective on the famous play. She picked up her laptop and searched for relevant books on the subject of the Salem Witch Trials. Two titles stood out – *The Salem Witch Trials* by Marilynne K. Roach and *In the Devil's Snare: The Salem Witchcraft Crisis of 1692* by Mary Beth Norton. Abi then went on to the *Abebooks* website and researched the cheapest second-hand copies she could find and ordered both titles, using her debit card for payment. This done, she then picked up her copy of Arthur Miller's *The Crucible* and settled down to read it.

There was a tap on her bedroom door. "Yes?" she queried. The door opened and her brother, Ben, was standing on the threshold.

"Jamie's dad has built him a brilliant treehouse!" he exclaimed.

Abi raised her eyebrows. "Am I bovved?" she asked.

"You should be, 'cos it means that I'm not interested in the stupid garden shed any more. You can have it," he stated, putting his hands in his pockets and waiting for his sister to thank him from the bottom of her heart.

"Okay, ta for that," was all she said as she turned her attention back to the textbook.

Ben tutted and noisily closed her bedroom door.

"Yesss!" Abi secretly congratulated herself. She was a lot more pleased with this turn of events than she had let on to Ben. It wouldn't do to let him see how much this meant to her as he wouldn't hesitate to change his mind. She sighed and picked up her book again.

Act One began with an overture... *A small upper bedroom in the home of Reverend Samuel Parris, Salem, Massachusetts, in the spring of the year 1692... His daughter Betty Paris, aged ten, is lying on the bed, inert.*

Abi was immediately hooked from the very beginning of the play. She read solidly for an hour, breaking off at intervals to make notes for future reference. Finally, she glanced at her bedside clock and saw, with a shock, that it was past ten o'clock and time for bed. Outside of her open bedroom window, the evening had gone from a golden sunset to darkness. Her curtains blew gently in the breeze and nearby, an owl hooted. She quickly got ready for bed, popped downstairs to say goodnight to her parents, visited the bathroom to clean her teeth and was in bed with the lights out by half past ten. She snuggled down between the sheets, letting her thoughts turn to Josh. She was convinced that he had held her hand a little longer than was needed and this thought brought a little warm flush to her cheeks. Oh, she could hardly wait for tomorrow and fell asleep while mentally going through her wardrobe.

The following morning dawned with a fabulous sunrise and the promise of another warm and sunny day. Abi had woken up later than she had planned. One glance at her watch on the bedside table told her it was already half past eight. She jumped out of bed and peered out through her bedroom window. Josh was already hard at work and he had Ben busily jabbering in his ear. After a quick shower, Abi decided to put on her denim shorts and a cool short-sleeved white cotton blouse which was patterned with red poppies and slipped her feet into red flip-flops. She pinned her long golden hair up into a bun, applied mascara to her lashes and, as she always felt she looked pale first thing in the morning, rubbed a little bit of rouge on her cheeks for colour. Satisfied with her appearance, she made her way downstairs, passing Nicola who was on her way up the stairs.

"Morning," Abi greeted her sister.

"Dad says that although we are having a garden pond, we won't be having any fish in it!" exclaimed Nicola, looking incredulous. "What is the point of a pond without fish?" she asked, and shaking her head, she carried on her journey upstairs without waiting for Abi to reply.

Abi shrugged her shoulders and made her way to the kitchen to grab some breakfast. Her mum and dad were sitting at the table, each enjoying a cup of tea. On seeing Abi, her mother indicated a plate of buttered toast. Abi picked up a piece.

"Nick's not happy – no fish in the pond she says," Abi looked at her dad.

"That's right. According to Alan Titchmarsh, fish pollute ponds. We want to attract frogs, toads and newts. We don't want or need any fish and we certainly don't need the cost of feeding them," said Robert, looking at his daughter.

"Okay," answered Abi, selecting another piece of toast.

"Ah! I wonder if Josh has had any breakfast? I'll just go and ask him if he would like some," said her mum.

"Mary, bring Ben in with you when you come back, please. It's time he and I were setting off for footie practice," said Robert. His wife nodded.

Suddenly, from the depths of the garden, there was a whoop of delight. 'Treasure!" yelled Ben. "Josh has dug up some treasure!"

Everyone rushed outside, including Nicola, who had come thumping down the stairs in her eagerness to see what all the fuss was about.

Gathered ringside and gazing down into the hole, the family could see what looked like a tin trunk being unearthed. Josh was working carefully to dig enough mud away so as to be able to prise the trunk free from its grave. Soon, he had exposed a couple of handles, one at each end of the trunk. He glanced up at Robert, hopeful of some help. It was Ben who jumped down and helped to hoist the trunk up out of the hole and on to the grass.

Everyone was silent as they took in the condition of the trunk. It was padlocked, which posed a problem, since there was no likelihood of there being a key anywhere close by.

"Shall I break the padlock with the spade?" enquired Josh. Robert nodded and so Josh chopped at the padlock. It took a couple of attempts but eventually the padlock broke in two. Inside, once the lid had been lifted, lay a large wooden doll and some things wrapped in John Lewis bags.

"Well, this trunk hasn't been down there all that long then," stated Mary, indicating the bags. "It's definitely not a cache of gold coins." She laughed.

"Ohhhh! It's like landing on the moon for the first time and finding an empty Coke can!" moaned a disappointed Ben. His dad ruffled his hair.

Abi and Nicola squatted down and began pulling the contents out of the trunk. Abi carefully lifted the wooden doll and thoughtfully studied it. The doll had been fashioned in the style of the Puritan era. In her left hand she carried a partly unwound scroll on which could be read the words *SEARCH THE SCRIPTURES [JOHN V.39]*. In her right hand, she carried a Bible. The expression carved into her face was, Abi thought, serene, but Nicola took one look at the doll and backed away, saying what an ugly, scary face it had.

"And look, Abi, she has no feet! Someone has chopped them off!" exclaimed Nicola. The rest of the family had a look and decided that the feet had indeed been chopped off.

"Someone doesn't want her getting about," stated Ben, creeping up behind Nicola and grabbing her. She jumped and let out a squeal. "Don't, Ben! She's evil! Dad, put her on the wood pile for burning!" Nicola demanded.

"What! No way!" Abi held the doll closer to her. "Leave her alone. I think she's quite lovely and I would like her as an ornament in my room, please." She looked at her mother for permission.

"Well," said Mary, "it seems that you are the only one that has taken to her so I guess she is yours. Although I suppose we ought to find out who she belonged to – it may be that she has been stolen and we should return it. I'll ask about in the village, see if I can find out anything. In the meantime, Abi, you can give her a good home, but don't get too attached in case you have to give her back. What's in the other packages?"

One of the bags contained a beautiful clear glass vase shaped like a teardrop and in the other bag there was a leather-bound book which had not fared well at all. Which was a shame. The book was mouldy and smelly and, whatever it had been about, was now illegible.

"I think that's had it," stated Robert, indicating the book. "It might as well go straight in the bin."

"Oh no," pleaded Abi, who loved books and couldn't bear the thought of throwing one away, even one in such a poor state as this one was. "I'll see what I can do with it."

"You'll have your work cut out," laughed Josh.

"Well, I'm going to give this a bit of TLC too," said Mary, picking up the vase and taking it into the house.

"Guess that leaves the rusty old trunk for me then," said Robert. "Okay, leave it there and I'll move it into the garage when we get back from footie training. Come on, young man," he said, tapping Ben on the head. "It's time we were off."

Father and son set off for the car, Mary went into the house with the vase, Nicola had already disappeared somewhere, so this just left Abi and Josh.

"Any ideas on all of this?" asked Abi.

"The doll looks as though she has been some religious icon at one time perhaps," suggested Josh, picking up his spade and jumping back down into the hole to continue digging. "I've nearly finished this digging. Reckon I've gone deep enough now to maybe lay the black sheeting. I'll assume that your dad will agree, so I'll level up the hole to make it a good shape for the next part of the process." Josh smiled at her.

Abi's legs turned to jelly. She scooped up the doll, which was about a metre in length, and also gently picked up the book. "I'm just going to put these things in my bedroom. Then I'll be back to see if you need any help," she said, smiling back.

Abi hurried up to her room with her prizes. She put the book on her desk to await further attention and stood the doll on her dressing table, balancing it against the wall. She would think of a more appropriate place later. Then she scooted back downstairs and was just flitting through the kitchen to the back door, when her mother, who was washing the vase at the sink in warm soapy water, asked if she wouldn't mind popping the kettle on and making some coffee for the two of them and Josh.

Annoyed, Abi did as she was told.

"He's rather a nice young man, don't you think?" asked her mum. "He's just finished his first year at uni and is spending the summer doing odd jobs to make a bit of money. He's staying with the vicar and his family. Has Michelle mentioned him? I think he's going out with Michelle's sister, Susie. They are at the same uni I believe. Probably how they met each other.'

This last bit of news, delivered it would seem, quite innocently by her mother, had the effect of destroying Abi's insides. She felt quite sick and more than a little like crying. *Don't be silly*, she chided herself. *You've only just met him, so how can you feel so devastated by this news?*

Nevertheless, she did. She made two cups of coffee instead of three.

"There you are." She indicated the mugs. "I don't know how *he* likes his coffee so I've left it black," and with that she went back up to her room and flopped on to her bed.

Back in the kitchen, Mary sighed to herself. She had wondered whether Abi was attracted to Josh. For one thing, she wasn't usually up so early on a Saturday morning. One didn't need to be Einstein to work out the reason for the carefully applied make-up and clothes. Abi was in the habit of slopping around in her pyjamas at the weekend. It was with a heavy heart that Mary had decided to burst Abi's bubble early on. She didn't want her daughter to become too attached to Josh and then find out that he was already spoken for. Not to mention that he was too old for her anyway. This last argument would not have been used, however, as no girl wanted to feel that she was too young. Sometimes it wasn't easy being a mum.

Abi was curled up in a ball on her bed. She didn't cry, although she felt like it. She was embarrassed because she felt she had been too obvious in her approach to Josh and that he was probably having a laugh to himself at her expense. But then again, she mused, what had she done, other than be polite, that could have alerted Josh to her interest in him? Nothing. She had done nothing. It was all in her head. Just because she knew how she felt didn't mean he had any idea. Once Abi had established this, she began to feel a little better. *Oh well*, she thought. *There are plenty more Joshes out there*. She was glad she hadn't contacted Michelle, though. At least her feelings were still secret. *Old feelings*, she corrected herself. The helium balloon that was David Smith faltered on the edge of space and wondered if it could return to the place in her heart. No. She had moved on from him too. In fact, she was going to be a 'boy-free' zone from now on and concentrate entirely on her homework – especially *The Crucible*.

Later that night, the family were all tucked up in their beds. The evening was quiet. No wind to speak of and a full moon casting its pearly light over the garden and in through chinks in curtains. Abi awoke with a start. She had been dreaming, but of what she couldn't be sure. Someone had been whispering in her ear, that much she could remember. She lay quietly in bed. Her bedroom had a strange atmosphere. A feeling of something about to happen. Over by her dressing table she could hear a faint rustling, as though pages of a book were being turned. She reached out and snapped on her bedside lamp. There was nothing there, but her bedroom window was open and the curtains were blowing very gently. Perhaps this was the cause of the rustling. Satisfied, Abi turned her light off and settled back down. A new noise came to the fore. The sound of someone walking around with an unusual cadence, as though whoever it was had to get around with the aid of two walking sticks. Abi listened, trying to pinpoint the area of the house the noise was coming from.

It was impossible to decide and she began to wonder if it was in her own head. She wondered what tinnitus – a constant vibration in the ear – sounded like. Maybe she had this. Eventually the noise died away and Abi was able to resume her sleep.

In the morning, however, she had a shock. The old, leather-bound book, which had nearly been thrown away the day before, was now a fully restored journal. Abi turned its pages and was amazed to find that it had been someone's diary. The book appeared to be extremely old because the date on the opening page was the 23rd September 1693.

Chapter Two

Abi quickly picked up the book and hurried downstairs to show the family. "Look!" she exclaimed excitedly. "The book for some reason has restored itself! Maybe it just had to dry out or something."

Robert looked at the book. It was still the mouldy, smelly mess it was yesterday. "Are you having a joke? It's in an awful condition!"

Abi frowned and took another look at the book. What was her father talking about? She looked at her mum. "Don't you think it looks a lot better than yesterday?" she asked.

Mary shook her head. "No, I don't, Abi. I think it's a health hazard!"

Abi looked at her brother and sister. They shook their heads, agreeing with their parents.

Abi couldn't understand it. The book was like new. All the writing, although written by an old-fashioned hand, was clearly legible. It was as though she was looking at something different than what they could see. She turned on her heel and took the book back up to her room. It didn't matter anyway. As long as she could read it. Why worry?

If they wanted to play dumb, that was up to them. She opened the journal at its first page.

Wednesday, 23rd September in the year 1693

I have been on my way travelling back to England for just one day. After all the happenings in Salem Village, Uncle Samuel has seen fit to send me back to live with my father's family. I know he blames me for everything. The ship set sail and soon ran into choppy waters and I confess I am suffering from sea sickness and am confined to my bed, or rather, to the pile of bedding that serves as it. To while away the time, I have decided to keep a journal of my recent past life and of my life as it unfolds from this day forward.

Where to begin? Well, I was born in Huntingdonshire, England, on the 12th July in the year of our Lord 1680. I was the only child of my parents. When I was around the age of nine years, we decided to travel to the New World and a better way of life. My parents were unhappy because they disagreed with the leading religions of the country and wanted to practice their faith in their own way. We were, and I am, Puritan. Our elders had already made their way across the water to a new life and we followed in their wake. My mother already had some family living there. Uncle Samuel Parris, who was, at that time, hoping to be the new reverend for Salem Village, was waiting to receive us...

Abi put down the journal and turned to the list of characters in her textbook of *The Crucible*. Yes, she was right! There was a character called the Reverend Samuel Parris! Could this be the journal of *Abigail Williams*? She opened her laptop and keyed in *Abigail Williams*. A quick scan through online details on *Abigail* revealed that no one knew what had become of her. Details of her had vanished from records and it was assumed that she had died sometime before 1697, but this was guesswork. If this journal was to be believed, then *Abigail* had returned to England in disgrace, it would seem. Abi was excited, although her mother's comments when the trunk had been unearthed, about the John Lewis bags and things not being that old, rang in her ears. Maybe the journal wasn't authentic after all. Also, why were these things buried in their garden? A coincidence or what, especially with her just beginning to study *The Crucible*. Even if the journal was a fake, Abi felt that it was still very interesting and could play a part in her new dramatisation for the Drama department. She continued to read from the journal.

Our journey to Salem Town was fraught. After disembarking the ship at Boston, we joined a party which was to pass through Salem en-route to further destinations. It was not a great distance to Salem. A mere twenty-four miles or so, which, on a good day, was just about a day's travel with steady walking. It is always safer to travel around in groups because of the threat of a Native American attack. There is a modicum of safety in numbers. The route we followed was forestry and dark with tall trees standing to attention either side. We noticed that the menfolk of our fellow travellers were tense and had a tendency to jump at any rustling of leaves or snapping of twigs underfoot. They carried their rifles at the ready. We were not long into our journey when Native American braves materialised between the trees. It put the fear of God into us. Mother and I, along with other wives and daughters, hid behind the heavily laden carts, and said our prayers. Father, eager to do his bit, went to join the menfolk, took aim and waited for the onslaught to begin. For a while, which seemed ages to me, no one moved and the air was thick with distrust. Suddenly, a group of horsemen could be heard coming closer. Friend or foe? The Native Americans vanished into the dark interior of the forest, just as silently as they had arrived. The reinforcements had come, in the form of a local army, from Boston. Apparently, shortly after our departure from Boston, the army had been warned, by a native informer, about a band of renegade braves which was carrying out random flash attacks on settlers. It was a miracle the men from Boston had arrived when they did as we had been greatly outnumbered by the natives. Afterwards, the army said they would accompany us as far as Salem Town, to keep us safe. We then carried on our journey as though nothing had happened. Which I found hard to understand. Mother, Father and I were terribly shaken but the families we were travelling with just brushed the incident off,

*saying there was a lot worse waiting out there and we
needed to toughen up!*

*There were no further problems on our stretch of the
journey and we were safely delivered to Salem Town.
Uncle Samuel met us as was promised and he took us to a
farmstead on the outskirts of Salem Village, a much
smaller community than Salem Town, but one that was
keen to shake off governance by the Town and become its
own master. The farmstead was in a lonely spot and in
need of much repair. A woman and her small son lived
there. Her husband had been killed by a Native American
tribe a year or so ago and she was struggling to keep up
with the farm. We were to help with the repairs and
planting of crops in return for bed and board. A solution
which suited all...*

Abigail had come to the end of the page in the journal
and so Abi put it to one side to read later. She was
enthralled. What a hard time those settlers had had, carving
out a new life for themselves. Abi had never appreciated
this before. She and her family had been to the USA for
holidays on a number of occasions and they were struck
by the seemingly 'milk and honey' atmosphere, never
giving it a thought as to how such an existence had been
achieved.

Her thoughts were disturbed by her mother yelling up
the stairs. "Abi! Do you want some breakfast before I clear
away the dishes? You had better have some now if you're
going to or else you won't want any Sunday lunch."

Abi had completely forgotten about her breakfast and now that she thought about it, she found that she was hungry. She got off of the bed and hurried to the door. As she opened it, her eyes fell on the wooden doll still propped up on her dressing table. *I'll give you some attention soon and think of a name for you,* she thought.

As Abi closed the door behind her, a voice whispered close to her ear. *"Peg... I'm called Peg."* She whirled around, looking for the source of the whisper, but there was no one or nothing that could be held responsible. Abi suddenly felt afraid up there on the landing all by herself. It was as though the rest of the family, although only downstairs, were a million miles away. She almost ran down the stairs, taking them two at a time, using the handrail and allowing her other hand to slide down the wall for extra balance. She arrived in the kitchen, still going at top speed.

Her mother looked at her in surprise. "Goodness me! I didn't mean that fast!" she exclaimed.

Abi shrugged her shoulders and sat down at the table, helping herself to some cereal. Now that she was no longer alone, she felt silly for having been afraid.

The smell of roasting beef permeated through the kitchen and intensified as Mary lifted the pan out of the oven and placed it on top of the hob. The fat was crackling and spitting as she basted the meat and then added the potatoes to roast in the meat juices. Abi's mouth was watering and she decided not to have any toast, the better to eat her lunch later.

"How's the pond coming along?" she asked her mum.

"It's a rest day," said Mary. "Josh has taken the time off and he and Susie have gone on a day trip somewhere."

At the mention of Josh, Abi momentarily closed her eyes in order to get command of her racing heart. She was annoyed that there was obviously still some interest buried in her subconscious. At least she could go into the garden without having to be aware of his nearness and tomorrow she would be back at school anyway.

"I'm going to investigate the shed," she announced.

"Well, be careful," warned her mum. "There will be all sorts of rubbish in there!"

Abi walked into the garden and down the path, through the trees and to the shed. Carefully she slid the big rusty bolt back and the door creaked open. Inside, a mammoth task awaited her. It was easy to see why no one had attempted to clear it out up to now. It was a daunting prospect. The shed was full of empty, mouldy boxes and other trash. Abi almost closed the door and walked away. However, she really wanted a private den to which she could invite her friends so she began the arduous job of clearing it out. She rolled her hair up into a bun and secured it with an elastic hair band which she always wore around her wrist for just such times when she didn't want her long locks flopping in her face.

She began by pulling the boxes out of the shed and dumping them on the ground. Amongst these boxes, there was a Ouija board, complete with a little heart-shaped planchette, which gave Abi an idea. She put the board and planchette to one side and continued with her sorting and cleaning. Surprisingly, when she had cleared the shed of the boxes, she could see that there were some wooden chairs. Encouraged, she lifted them out and was left with an empty space which needed a good sweep and dust. Cobwebs were everywhere. Abi was squeamish about spiders but managed to push her fear away. She was too determined to provide a tidy den to let spiders stop her. She started by brushing the cobwebs away from the window. Then she began sweeping the floorboards. Dust rose up like a choking cloud all around her and she had to abandon the shed for some fresh air outside. She emerged coughing and spluttering. Her mum was waiting outside with a bucket of water.

"Here, Abi," said Mary, laughing. "It's best to damp the dust down before you start sweeping," she continued, and she began to sprinkle water over the floor of the shed and then took the brush and carried on sweeping. Soon the shed looked clean.

"Come on now," ordered Mary. "Lunch is nearly ready and you should leave the floor to dry for a bit. I have an old rug which you can have. I'll look it out after we've had our meal."

Abi nodded and followed her mum back to the house. She was very hungry after her exertions.

Later in the afternoon, Abi and Mary completed the finishing touches to the shed. Mary had found the old rug and also some old curtains. Robert had put up a rail over the window and the curtains, which had rings for hooks, were threaded over the rail. Abi was so pleased with the result. The curtains were able to be pulled closed and open without trouble. Together they polished the four chairs before placing them in the shed. Nicola and Ben donated the big beanbag seats they had in their bedrooms and which they no longer wanted. Abi was grateful to them, especially Ben, as she could see that he now wished he had kept pushing for the shed for himself. He and Jamie had fallen out over something and were not talking to each other at the moment so Ben was not invited to the tree house. Abi felt this argument would soon be resolved as Ben and Jamie had been friends for most of their lives.

All five of the family then broke up the mouldy boxes and put them in the recycle bin, pushing them well down, so other 'green' rubbish would fit in. There was still another week to go before the recycle bin would be emptied.

After tea, a snack affair of scones, raspberry jam and clotted cream, Abi went to her room to finish off her maths, history and science homework. She then turned her attention to *The Crucible*. Nicola popped her head around the door to ask about the wooden doll.

"Have you done anything with her yet, Abi? You know, polished her and found somewhere proper for her to live?" asked Nicola.

Abi looked up from her text book. "No, I haven't yet," she admitted. She went over to the dressing table and picked up the doll. "Can you go downstairs, please, and get a cloth and we'll give her a bit of a dust?" she asked her sister.

Nicola hurried down to the cupboard where their mother kept all of the household cleaning materials. She selected a soft, clean, cloth and raced back to Abi's room. Together the girls sat on the bed and dusted the doll.

"Oh!" exclaimed Abi. "There's a little hanging bracket which has been tapped into her back. I've not noticed that before."

"Looks like she was hung up on a wall, perhaps," suggested Nicola.

"Hmm… I know where to put her now!" said Abi enthusiastically. "There is a nail in the wall over there which has nothing hanging from it at the moment. I think she would look good hanging over there."

Nicola surveyed the potential position of the new home for the doll. "That means you would be able to see her from your dressing table mirror. Her reflection will be behind you when you are sitting at it."

"What's wrong with that?" asked Abi

Nicola shook her shoulders. "Nothing, I guess. It just seems creepy to me. I don't like the doll. She has an atmosphere about her. I know she's carrying a scroll and the Bible, but even so, she scares me."

"You've been watching too many horror films," laughed Abi.

Nicola didn't rise to this. She had been in enough trouble when she had had nightmares after watching *The Blair Witch Project*. "Are you going to give her a name?"

Abi nodded. "Her name is Peg, or Peggy."

"Where have you dreamt that name up from?" asked Nicola, frowning.

"It just popped into my head earlier," replied Abi, not mentioning the whispering voice she had heard. She had just teased Nicola about being scared so she could hardly admit to having been frightened herself.

"Nick!" their mum's voice could be heard calling up the stairs. "Time to be getting ready for bed. School tomorrow."

Nicola made a face and rolled off the bed. "Night night, Abi. See you in the morning."

Abi blew her sister a kiss and turned her attention to hanging the doll on the nail. She stood back to admire her choice of position. Happy with it, she went back to her text book and continued reading.

At around half past nine, she yawned and decided it was time for her to go to bed. She sat at her dressing table, removed her make-up and took down her hair, which was still caught up in the quick bun she had fashioned earlier when starting to clear out the shed. She was really pleased with the end result of the shed and couldn't wait to invite some friends over. Maybe they could start some secret club and the shed could be their meeting place.

The following morning Abi caught the bus along with Michelle. The day was grey and cool, which wasn't surprising as they were well into the month of October. So far, autumn had been very warm but it looked as though the weather had finally turned.

"Did you have a nice weekend, Abi?" asked Michelle, as the bus pulled away from the village stop.

Abi nodded. "Not too bad, thanks. I cleared out the shed and made it habitable. I'm really pleased with it."

Michelle watched her friend as though waiting for some revelation. When Abi said nothing more, Michelle frowned.

"Did you meet Josh then? I thought you would have been full of it, telling me all about the hottie who is digging out your pond!" She laughed.

At the mention of Josh, Abi felt herself tense up. She didn't want to talk about him and she certainly didn't want to hear all about him and Susie. "Oh... Him," she said as nonchalantly as she could. "Is he a hottie? I hadn't noticed."

Michelle was surprised. "You did speak to him though, didn't you? He said he had met you. It's the first time we've met him. We knew Susie had met someone at uni', but we didn't know much about him until now. He's really nice."

"Yes, I spoke to him, briefly, but that was all," replied Abi.

Michelle glanced at Abi. There was something not quite right. Her friend seemed unusually reticent. "Did something happen, Abi? Did he overstep the mark, or something?" she asked.

Abi just wanted to change the subject. She had a strange feeling in her throat which seemed to be preventing her from speaking. She shook her head and turned her attention to looking out of the window. The bus had pulled in to another stop to pick up more school children. Several were getting on, including Ricky Morris. He saw her watching and grinned.

Michelle was worried. Was Josh not all that he seemed? She was concerned for her sister, Susie. It was obvious to Michelle that Abi was not telling her something so her imagination began to run rife.

Abi remained distant towards Michelle for the rest of the day. It was a new atmosphere between the two girls, one that Michelle found hard to handle. They had never kept secrets from each other before.

That night, as Abi was getting ready for bed, she reflected on her attitude over the question of Josh. She knew that Michelle was letting her imagination run away with herself and as a result was beginning to draw the wrong conclusions and Abi had to admit that she liked the idea that her friend was now suspicious of Josh. *I won't say anything else*, thought Abi. *I'll just let her think that maybe Josh can't be trusted.*

Even so, Abi's conscience pricked her, as she was normally a very fair and honest person, but something about the whole Josh situation had made her take leave of her senses so she shut out her conscience. *It's only a bit of fun*, she told herself.

As she brushed her hair, her gaze caught the reflection in the mirror of the wooden doll hanging on the wall. *She looks perfect hanging over there*, thought Abi, weaving her hair into a large single plait and securing the end with the hair band.

"Do you remember how I used to brush your hair Abigail?" whispered a voice close to Abi's ear. She jumped and dropped the brush on the floor. Looking fearfully around her, Abi hurried to her bedroom door and threw it open, half expecting, hoping even, that it was Ben playing tricks. No one was there. There wasn't even a hint of anyone having been there. There was darkness coming from under the closed doors of both Ben and Nicola, suggesting that they were both asleep. Her parents' door stood open and the bedroom was eerily dark as they were both still downstairs. Abi closed her door and looked around her own room. Nothing had changed – the brush was on the floor and her used make-up wipe rolled up in a ball on the dressing table top was still waiting to be thrown in the bin. She then heard the reassuring noise of her parents locking up for the night, preparing to come to bed, so she hurried up and went to the bathroom to clean her teeth. She was keen to use their nearness to drive away the irrational fear that was trickling along her spine.

When she returned to her room, she felt much better. She heard her parents moving around in their room and felt safe. *It's all in my imagination*, she told herself, getting into bed and snapping off the light.

Much later she was awakened by that sound of someone walking around with the use of walking sticks. She lay in her bed sweating, not daring to move. Then, very softly, came another whisper. *"Abigail! Where are you?"* and a light warm air, like someone's breath, washed over her face.

Abi sat up and clicked on her lamp. Lovely, friendly light banished the evil, all-consuming darkness, yet Abi was still afraid. Her brush, which she was sure she hadn't picked up from the floor, was now back on the dressing table and the hair which was always wrapped around the bristles had been pulled from it and was left in a little furry ball by the side of the brush.

Abi swallowed nervously. She was uncertain what to do. Maybe she had unconsciously picked up the brush and pulled the hair from it? If not, what was the alternative reason? She dared not answer this question. She decided to sleep with her light on. She felt safer.

Chapter Three

The date of Halloween was arriving fast. Normally Abi and her brother and sister dressed up and went 'trick or treating' around the village, stopping at people's houses who were happy to join in. Not everyone wanted trick or treaters banging on their doors and some residents were totally against what they viewed as a nasty 'Americanism' which had infiltrated British customs. Michelle, being the daughter of the vicar, was not allowed to accompany her friend on what her father felt was nothing more than a pagan event.

This year, however, Abi decided that she would invite some friends over and they would have a séance in the shed, using the Ouija board she had unearthed. Lately, she was feeling braver as there had been no further 'weird' things happening at night and so she put it all down to an over-imaginative mind. Why, she might even have an oomancy – like the girls in Salem Village. She could use the tear-shaped clear glass vase, which her mother had filled with dried rose petals and popped on Abi's windowsill. Abi's books, which she had ordered from AbeBooks a little while ago, had arrived. Two great big tomes which the postman had struggled to carry up to the front door. She had begun reading them. It was not certain that the girls of Salem Village had dabbled with oomancy, but Abi felt that, as young females interested in their futures, to them, the forbidden oomancy would have been a delicious, potentially dangerous and underhanded way of entertaining themselves, and so Abi, as a fellow young female, was convinced that they had used the "egg white and hot water in a clear glass" routine.

At school, Abi screwed up her courage and asked a group of girls to her Halloween party to be held in her shed. These girls were considered, both by themselves and others, to be super cool. Michelle and herself were only tolerated on the very fringe of the group, sometimes included in its social events and sometimes not.

"Sharon, would you and the others like to come to my Halloween party I'm having in my newly decorated shed?

Sharon stopped whispering to her gang of close friends. She raised her eyebrows and Abi found herself waiting for a sarcastic reply. One of the other girls let out a giggle.

"Okay," Sharon eventually replied. "Should be good fun," she continued with a sideways glance at her tribe. They looked bemused but nodded their heads in agreement nonetheless. "What time shall we arrive?"

"Shall we say seven-fifteen?" suggested Abi. Sharon agreed and then went back to chatting to her crowd. Abi took this as a dismissal and left them to it. She spied

Michelle walking past the classroom door and headed out into the corridor to catch her up.

"I've just invited Sharon and her crew to my Halloween party I'm having in the shed!" she exclaimed.

Michelle looked at Abi aghast. "Have you lost your mind? It will have to be a good party or you might have just committed social suicide!

"Possibly," Abi replied, her feelings, which, only five minutes ago had been on a high, sinking fast. "You'll come though, Michelle, won't you? Please?" she implored.

"You know my dad doesn't like me taking part in Halloween, Abi," she answered with a quick glance at her friend. She saw Abi become quite crestfallen. "Okay, okay, I'll see what I can do. I'll have to make up an excuse or something. Perhaps I can say you have invited me for a sleepover?"

"Yes! That's a good idea anyway. Stay after the party. We haven't done that in ages!" agreed Abi.

"I just hope you appreciate it, that's all. I don't like telling fibs to my dad."

The night of the Halloween party came around quickly. Abi had decorated the shed with fake cobwebs and creepy-looking black bats and bought lots of Halloween sweets and treats. She had found a small round table with a pedestal leg and drop sides in the Sue Ryder charity shop in Huntingdon. It wasn't too expensive so she had purchased it. With the drop sides fully extended, the table would be excellent for them all to gather round for the séance. Abi could hardly wait. Although, she had to admit to herself that she was very nervous. What if the evening was a flop? Maybe Michelle was right. Maybe she was about to socially destroy herself.

At least she wouldn't have to worry about her brother Ben spoiling things. He had his own plans for the evening. Something to do with Jamie and the treehouse. Ben and Jamie were back to being friends. Whatever had caused their break-up had been resolved. Although, Abi reflected, Ben wasn't himself. He was very quiet and subdued, as though something was on his mind. Abi made a mental note to have a talk with him. He usually got on her nerves but she did care about him and if he needed someone to talk to, then she would make herself available.

In his bedroom, Ben looked through his window and could just make out, in the deepening dusk, his sister shutting the shed door, her preparations complete. He hoped her little party was a success. He turned his attention to his own evening's plans. Jamie wanted everyone to arrive at the treehouse for seven o'clock. Ben wasn't looking forward to Jamie's plans. He thought the plans were cruel. They involved teasing one of the village's oldest inhabitants, an old lady who lived by herself and who was hardly ever seen and who had, on one occasion, told Jamie off for trespassing.

One day, so Jamie had explained to Ben and the rest of the gang when they were sitting in the treehouse, Jamie had been kicking his ball along the road when he accidentally kicked it over the old lady's fence and into her garden. He had peered over the fence but he could not see where his ball had come to rest as the garden was a wilderness, so he had entered the garden and searched for it. He soon found it, but instead of leaving the garden quickly, he decided to look around. He soon lost interest in the garden and turned his attention to peeping through the windows of the house. Suddenly, the back door of the house flew open and out came the old lady, shaking her fist and telling Jamie to clear off. Jamie said he had been scared. He had turned tail and ran as fast as he could out of the garden and back home. Once there, after he had calmed down, he vowed he would get even with the old lady. The idea that maybe the old lady had a point and that Jamie should not have been in the garden didn't even occur to him. He was consumed with hatred. *Silly old bat,* he had thought to himself and he had visited the garden several times since, knocking on the front door, running round to the back of the house and throwing pebbles at the windows. The old lady never reappeared and he could imagine her cowering in fright somewhere in the depths of her house and the thought pleased him. Gave him a sense of power.

When Jamie's dad had finished constructing the treehouse, Jamie had started a club. The members of this club were made up of his closest friends and, of course, Ben was the oldest friend he had and so Jamie made Ben his deputy. At first Ben had been proud, but as Jamie began to recount his actions to the members regarding the old lady and to outline his plans for making her life an even bigger misery, Ben had spoken up, saying he thought it all too spiteful and couldn't they focus on something more productive for the club? Jamie had turned quite nasty. Ben had never seen this side to his friend before. They had argued and the other members had not backed Ben at all. To be fair, they had not particularly supported Jamie either. They had just remained mutely sitting on the floor with legs crossed and their eyes downcast, waiting for the row to be over. It had ended with Jamie shouting that if Ben couldn't or wouldn't support the club's plans, then he could clear off. Ben had jumped up off the floor and climbed down the treehouse rope ladder and stomped off home.

The next day, at school, Ben was to fully understand the extent of his exile from the club. None of his friends would talk to him and he had spent a very lonely week. Not wanting to be seen as a loser, he had sought out Jamie and patched things up, stating that he was willing to participate fully in the club's activities. Jamie had welcomed him back. However, deep down, Ben was not happy and he knew that what they were going to be doing was very wrong.

Ben sighed and moved away from his window. He felt not at all like himself. Normally he was full of life and ready for the next adventure, but at the moment he felt depressed and very uncertain about his feelings.

Later that evening, Michelle arrived around six-thirty, just enough time for her to drop off her overnight bag in Abi's room and to get dressed in suitable Halloween clothing. She and Abi had decided to dress up as goths and they had bought themselves jet black wigs. . Once they were ready, they headed downstairs to await the guests.

Esther Abelman looked at her watch and frowned. He was late tonight. For a moment she clutched at the thought that he wasn't going to bother her this evening, but then she remembered that it was Halloween. He obviously had something extra planned for her.

Esther sat down and rested her head in her hands. He was a little brat who had no respect for someone her age. He needed a good clip round the ear. She was scared of him. How far would he take things? The first time he had been to her house after she had told him off, he had banged on her front door, shouted verbal abuse through her letter box then had gone off round the back of her house and started throwing pebbles at her windows. The whole episode took her right back. Right back to when she was a little girl, living in Berlin just before the outbreak of war. She could remember the fear she and her family felt every night as people she had known all her life had turned against them and came armed with bricks which they hurled through their windows and daubed '*juden*' in paint on their front door. Her father had realised quickly that the situation for their people was only going to get much worse and so, with good insight as it turned out, he had managed to get himself and his family to England, where he had a cousin who was able to help them start over. They had settled well into their new surroundings and as the horrors of the war unfolded and the terrible findings of the final solution came to light, they were immensely grateful and thankful that they had had the foresight to leave when they did.

Esther had thought that she would never again have to face such persecution. Whilst she appreciated that the boy was not abusing her because she was Jewish, he was, nevertheless, persecuting her because of her age and because she was all alone and because he could. There was no one she could turn to. She didn't have a family, and she didn't venture out much these days. One of her good friends had passed away, whilst the other had recently gone into a care home. She had wondered whether to ring the police, but worried that they would think her pathetic, bothering them with such a trivial problem when they had far worse to deal with. She felt utterly powerless. Esther glanced at her watch again and came to a decision. She couldn't stay in the house that night and be transported back to the fear she had known as a child. Quickly, or rather, as fast as she could these days, she pushed herself up from the sofa and collected some warm clothes and a duvet cover from her bed. In the kitchen, she made herself a flask of tea and packed up some sandwiches and threw in an apple. She had to act swiftly as she didn't want to risk running into the brat as she made her escape from her home. She had an idea where she could spend the night. It wasn't ideal but anything was going to be better than being forced to listen to the kind of language and antics that boy could produce.

Abi welcomed Sharon and her friends and together they went down the garden and to the shed. The other girls were decked out in a variety of horror costumes and they all looked like a 'motley bunch', as Abi's dad had said, when he saw them in the hallway. He requested that they keep the noise down and not to be too late as there was school tomorrow. Abi shot a quick, guarded look at Sharon. Her face conveyed the message that he had no right in telling them what to do as she considered they were too old for that kind of lecture. Abi bit her lip. Not a good start to the evening.

Abi opened the shed door. An eerie half-light shone within and the place did look creepy.

"Oh wow!" exclaimed Sharon and the others agreed. "I'm impressed. You must have worked hard to achieve this!" and she smiled at Abi.

Michelle nudged Abi in the back as an unspoken cheer of support. Perhaps the evening would be fun after all.

The goodies and cans of Coca-Cola Abi had put together in an old barrel she had found in the garage and moved to the shed. She told everyone to help themselves and they didn't need asking twice, plunging their hands in and finding packets of crisps and fruity chews. When they had eaten enough for the time being, Abi suggested they take up positions around the table so they could have a go at contacting the 'other side' with the use of the Ouija board and planchette. She stressed that they had to try and produce the right atmosphere, so they needed to be quiet and focus their attention. All the girls complied and when Abi felt the time was right, she urged them to each put one of their hands on to the planchette which was sitting in the middle of the board.

"Can you hear me? Does anyone wish to make contact?" asked Abi of the 'other world'. There was silence... but then suddenly the shed shook with a large bang, as though something outside had smacked into the side of it. All inside jumped and screamed. Sharon looked at Abi to see if this was something which had been arranged and was surprised to see that Abi was looking terrified, as was Michelle. *Oh!* thought Sharon. *This is deliciously scary!*

Outside, something was scratching at the walls and moaning, *Let me in.*

Esther Abelman slid out of her front door and locked it behind her. It was dark and the few street lamps that there were only gave out a minimal glow. She glanced around fearfully and was relieved to find that no one was around. She walked for a short distance along the road then cut down a footpath and headed into the woods. Her bag of provisions for the evening was quite heavy and cumbersome. In the dark, it kept snagging on the undergrowth and it slowed her progress. Determinedly, she carried on, telling herself that this was her way of taking back control.

Eventually, she came to her destination. The shed in the garden of her recently deceased friend. Her other friend had lived next door. The same friend who had recently gone into a care home and whose house was now empty. Esther knew the shed had recently been tidied up. She had overheard some talk about it whilst waiting to buy one or two things from the village shop. The mother of the new family who had moved in a short while ago was saying how her daughter had made a good job of making the shed look inviting.

Instead of making a beeline for the shed, Esther stood for a while, under cover of the trees, and watched for any signs of life. There was a curious glow coming from within and she wondered what was causing it. The cold air was beginning to make her shiver and so she decided to make a move. As she started to set off, she got into a muddle with the undergrowth, her bag, and a random sweeping brush which was lurking among this year's autumn leaves, and ended up falling over. A branch scratched her forehead and she could feel blood trickling down one side of her face.

Meanwhile, inside the shed, the girls were very quiet, each holding their breath. They had been sitting like that for the last ten minutes or so. Whatever had been scratching and moaning, had stopped. There was silence.

"I think maybe it has gone," said Abi, tentatively exhaling.

"Whatever 'it' was," replied Michelle.

"Are you sure you didn't have anything to do with that?" asked Sharon, regarding them through suspicious eyes.

Abi and Michelle shook their heads. "I've got no idea what that was! I honestly did not set that up!" exclaimed Abi.

Mandy, another of Sharon's crew and who was sitting directly opposite the shed window, was just lifting her can of coke to her mouth. Suddenly she let out a scream.

"There's a face with blood on it staring in through the window!" she yelled. The others turned their attention to where she was pointing and were just in time to see something disappear from view.

Mandy looked really frightened.

Outside of the shed, poor Esther ducked down and managed to get back under cover. She fully expected the shed door to fly open and for the girls to come out and check around. Of course! It was Halloween and they were having some sort of creepy gathering and Esther had managed, inadvertently, to add to the horror. Despite her predicament, Esther chuckled to herself. To her amazement, the shed door did not fly open. Instead, it creaked open very slowly and several heads poked out and looked around, before the girls quickly left the shed and scurried up the garden path towards the house. They looked quite a sight, witches and goths all running away, scared witless. They had had enough. It was too scary and they wished that they had not dabbled with the Ouija board. Abi was worried that it was all somehow connected to whatever had been manifesting itself ever since the trunk had been dug up. She was very glad that Michelle was staying over tonight.

In Esther's garden, however, the boys had arrived. Led by Jamie, they had entered by the front gate, with a reluctant Ben bringing up the rear. Jamie did his customary knocking on the front door. He then lifted up the flap of her letter box and sent an enormous burp echoing through it. "Hello, old lady. It's me. I've brought some friends along tonight!" He laughed and turned his attention back to his gang.

The house was in complete darkness. Somewhere in its depths, a phone started ringing. It went unanswered.

"Come on, she's obviously not here, so let's go. There's no point in teasing her if she's not here!" argued Ben.

Jamie glared at him. "You having second thoughts again?"

Ben shook his head and they continued their trek round to the back garden. Ben looked around. The old lady had neighbours, so how come no one noticed that she was being visited by a bully every night? *Bullies,* thought Ben.

That's what we are, and he hated himself for not standing up for what was right. Jamie, meanwhile, started throwing the eggs he had brought along, raided from his mum's kitchen, at the windows. One by one they hit the glass panes, smashed and dribbled the yellow yolk, mixed with bits of shell, down the length of the windows. The others thought this great fun and soon joined in. All except Ben. Unnoticed, he slipped away, back round to the front of the house and out of the gate. Once outside the property, he deliberated with himself for a few moments. Then, his mind made up, he walked to the old lady's next-door neighbour and banged on their front door and aggressively rang their doorbell. Anything, really, to get their attention. He ran away and hid before anyone came to the door. He fervently hoped that they would hear the noise coming from the old lady's back garden and realise that something was wrong and do something about it.

The girls reached the back door of Abi's house. Sharon was on her mobile, asking her dad to come and pick them up. At Abi's invitation to come into the house, she declined, saying that they would start walking home and meet up with her dad somewhere along the way. Sharon and her crew then carried on walking up the front garden path, passing Nicola, who was on her way home after her evening of trick or treating, complete with a pillowcase full of goodies.

"Well, I'm going to be a laughing stock tomorrow at school," said Abi, frowning. "That didn't go as I had planned."

"I'm not so sure," answered Michelle. "They were really scared and I don't think they will want to admit too much to that, so you may be okay."

Abi nodded and held up her crossed fingers. She turned her attention to Nicola. "Did you have a good time?"

Nicola nodded, holding up her bag of treats. "Not so sure about Ben though. I saw him hanging around by himself and he didn't look happy," she said, shrugging her shoulders.

"I hope he and Jamie haven't fallen out again!" replied Abi worriedly.

The girls went in through the back door. Abi's mum, Mary, asked them if they would like a drink of hot chocolate before bed. They all agreed, realising that they were quite chilly after their outside antics.

Mary went into the kitchen and poured some milk into a pan. Just as she was doing this, Ben came home and was asked if he would like some hot chocolate. He declined, saying he was tired and going straight to bed. He disappeared up the stairs, taking them two at a time. Everyone glanced at each other. It was obvious to them, given his red, puffy eyes, that he had been crying. Mary looked at Abi, a question forming in her eyes.

"Leave him, Mum," said Abi. "I'll have a word with him in a bit, when he's not so upset," she continued.

Mary nodded her agreement. "Keep me in the loop though, won't you?" she both asked and stated. Abi agreed.

Later, when Abi and Michele had retired to Abi's room for the night, the girls had a conversation as to what could be the matter with Ben. Abi glanced at the wooden doll which was hanging from its hook. Michelle followed her friend's glance. "Oh, is that the doll Josh was telling us about? He said something about digging up an old trunk in your garden when he was helping construct your pond."

"Yes, it is," answered Abi. Once again, she had tensed when Josh was mentioned. "How is Josh by the way? I haven't seen him since he finished working on our pond," she asked, curiosity getting the better of her.

"He and Susie have gone back to uni' for the start of the new academic year," Michelle replied. "I have to ask, Abi, did something happen which made you feel uncomfortable? Only, you seemed not like yourself whilst he was working at yours."

Abi thought for a moment. Michelle was her very best friend and had been for most of her life. They were more like sisters and it was hard to remember that they were not related. With another glance at the wooden doll, she decided to tell Michelle everything that had been happening since the exhumation of the trunk.

"I lied when I said I hadn't really noticed Josh. I came home from school and saw him working on the pond. I watched him for a while from the back gate and I thought he was so hot and I just wanted him to notice me. I thought he had, but then I found out, from Mum, that he was Susie's boyfriend and I just felt so silly, because I had really put myself out there, and I felt he would be laughing at me and telling Susie, and even you, about how I had acted like the silly schoolgirl I am. I couldn't talk about it and I had this kind of stiffness of jaw, as though something was trying to keep my mouth shut. Then, when I could see you were suspicious of him, I felt pleased and decided to let you carry on having your doubts about him. It was strange, I've never felt vindictive before but I did then and it felt good, made me feel as though I had managed to get the upper hand," explained Abi, a tear running down her face.

"I get why you would have felt like you did," said Michelle, after a moment's pause. "But Josh didn't say anything or appear as though he knew you were in to him, so your silly feeling was all in your mind. It was spiteful of you to let me think Josh had done something, though. But, in a funny way, I can understand that too. I'm just glad that I don't have to say to Susie that I think Josh is suss."

"I'm sorry, 'Shell," Abi apologised. "Are we okay?"

Michelle nodded and smiled. She turned her attention to the journal lying on the bedside table. She picked it up. Abi watched her and said nothing about its condition. She wanted to get Michelle's take on whether it was legible or not.

"Ugh! Are you hoping to be able to read this? It's in a terrible state. What a shame!" said Michelle, putting the book back and rubbing her hands in distaste.

Abi was disappointed. Michelle seemed to be as blind as the rest of her family. Undaunted, she, nevertheless, began to explain all of the creepy things which had happened since the trunk had been found. She told Michelle about the whispering and the hairbrush incident and demonstrated, by reading a little from the journal, that to her at least, the book was in a readable condition.

Michelle turned to look at the wooden doll. To her, it had a serene face and none of the atmosphere about it that Abi, and apparently her sister, Nicola, could feel. It was just a doll made of wood, hanging from a hook on the wall. "I'm sorry, Abi," she said, "but I think you are letting your imagination run away with you. Take her down if she bothers you, and put her away somewhere. Nick's suggestion of putting her on the log pile for burning is a good one!"

"Oh, I couldn't do that! She's a work of art! Anyway, my mum's going to ask some questions around the village to see if anyone can shed light as to who she may have belonged to. So I may have to give her back. She may of course have belonged to my great grandma, who used to live here before she died."

Michelle nodded. "As for this," and she indicated the journal. "I'm not sure what to make of it. You seem to be really reading the passages in it and not making it up as you go. I watched your eyes and they were moving along as though you were reading a normal book! Yet, I can't make out any of the words. And *Abigail Williams*! The *Abigail Williams!*"

"I know! It's bizarre! And at a time when we are writing our plays about *The Crucible* as well!" agreed Abi.

"Hmmm…" said Michelle, pondering. "The woman who used to live next door to this cottage had to go into a care home a few months ago. She fell and broke her hip and can no longer look after herself. Mentally she is as bright as a button, but physically her body has let her down. Anyway, she was really good friends with your dad's grandma and another old lady who lives in the village, Esther Abelman. Maybe these two ladies can help solve the mystery of the trunk?"

Outside, it had become windy and cold. Once all the fleeing witches had disappeared and the commotion had died down, Esther revisited the shed. In their haste to get away, the girls had left the door unlocked. In fact the padlock had come off and was lying on the muddy ground. Esther picked it up and pocketed it. She had to admit that she hadn't given it a thought that the newly cleaned shed might have a lock on it. It never used to have one when her friend Jean owned it. Esther's stomach rumbled, reminding her that she hadn't yet eaten and she entered the shed with the hope of settling down for the night. However, the wind blew harder and the shed seemed to rock and it was cold, damn it. Too cold. Her face was still bleeding and she needed some water to clean herself up.

She couldn't stay in the shed, but there was no way she was tramping back home tonight.

An idea occurred to her. The empty cottage next door might provide a safe place for tonight. Esther knew the secret place where Muriel had kept a spare key. Maybe it was still there? It was worth a look.

Chapter Four

Abi entered her classroom, the following morning, with trepidation. Everyone seemed to be looking at her.

"Here she is, Hinchingbrooke's answer to Mystic Meg!" exclaimed one of the boys, grinning.

"Respect!" said someone else. "Sharon had a great time last night. Says you laid on a really creepy show!"

Abi was amazed at the response. Ricky Morris was sitting on a desk nearby, and was busily tuning his guitar. He and his friends had formed a rock group, called *The Fen Tigers* and they were to perform before the school years nine to thirteen in assembly that morning. He did a thumbs up sign and winked.

Suddenly the penny dropped. "It was you, wasn't it? asked Abi. "You did the bang and scratching on the side of the shed!"

Ricky got up from the desk, placing his guitar safely on it, and responded with a low bow. "Guilty as charged!" he said and then moved her out through the classroom door, so they could have some privacy. "But don't be telling everyone. Let them think you successfully contacted the *'other side'*, " he continued.

"But why? asked Abi, frowning. "Why would you bother and how did you even know about the séance?"

"Why did I bother? Hmm… Let me think," replied Ricky, putting his finger to his chin and looking up to the ceiling for an answer. "Oh, I remember, it's cos I like you Abi and I wanted to help."

Abi blushed. "But how did you even know?

"I overheard Sharon and that lot talking about it and they were planning on rubbishing anything you did on the night. You would have been humiliated. I didn't want that to happen, so me and some friends got together and hid in the woods by your shed. You know, your back garden is a bit open to anyone who wants to come to your house via the woods. They would be straight in to your garden. There are no fences to keep anyone out!" he exclaimed.

Abi nodded. "My dad is going to do something about that when he can find the time. We have to find out, via the deeds to the property, just where our boundary ends. These things all take time." She paused. Something was bothering her. She was glad it had only been Ricky messing about and not a resurfacing of the weird events from a few weeks ago, but still, there was something else. "Oh I remember! Whose was the face with the blood on it who looked in through the window, then? That was a creepy touch to the evening!"

Ricky shrugged his shoulders. "I don't know what you mean. We did the bang and the scraping with the brush, which, incidentally, we just left the brush lying around, but that was it. Then we left quickly as we didn't want to be found out. There was no face with blood on it. If there was, it had nothing to do with us!"

Abi felt her stomach plummet. "What's up?" asked Ricky, noticing that Abi's complexion had turned pale.

"I'm scared, Ricky. Ever since a trunk was dug up in our garden, there have been some strange things going on," she explained.

The bell rang for registration and form time, after which they all filed along to the school hall for assembly. The usual 'sermon' from the Headmaster was delivered and then school notices were read out. Then it was time for the performance. The curtains behind where the teachers and Headmaster were sitting, on stage, were drawn back to reveal *The Fen Tigers,* who were in position and ready to play. Ricky was lead guitarist and lead vocalist. There were another two guitarists, one keyboard player and a drummer. The song they performed had been a hit , by Noel Gallagher's High-Flying Birds. It was one of Abi's favourite songs, and *The Fen Tigers* performed it well. Abi was surprised at how good they were, in particular Ricky. His eyes seemed to seek her out in the audience.

After assembly was over, she met him in the corridor and congratulated him on the performance. He was pleased to hear that she was so taken with their rock group. On a sudden impulse, Abi invited Ricky to come home with her that night after school so that she could explain the weird happenings properly. Ricky agreed. Secretly, he was delighted that Abi had invited him. Things were looking up!

In another classroom, Ben was already sitting at his desk. He was dreading Jamie arriving. After he had alerted the neighbours to the boys' antics in the back garden, he hadn't hung around and so he had no idea as to how the events unfolded.

The form teacher came in, armed with her registration book, and closed the door. Jamie had still not arrived. In fact, now that he thought about it, neither had the other club members.

There was a tap on the form room door and one of the sixth formers came in, brandishing a note, which was handed over to the teacher, Mrs Bryant, who unfolded and read it. She looked up and straight at Ben.

"Ben, you have been requested to go to the headmaster's room, please. Marcia will take you," and she indicated the sixth former who was waiting. "Better take your lesson books for the morning with you, then you can go straight to the relevant classroom when the headmaster has finished with you," she continued.

Ben picked up his bag and slung it over his shoulder. He had an inkling as to what the summons might be about. He followed Marcia along the corridor to the headmaster's room and after knocking on the door, they were told to enter.

Inside, sitting on chairs, were Jamie and his mum and dad, the other members of the club with their parents and Ben's mum and dad. Ben hardly dared meet the gaze of his parents. They would be so disappointed at having to come along to the school and at short notice too. His dad would have had to take time off work. He would not be impressed.

Ben wasn't sure what to expect. Was he one of the bullies, or was he a hero for being a whistle blower? He glanced at Jamie, but Jamie was slouched in his chair and looking down at his hands.

"It has been brought to my attention that this group of boys were found intimidating an old lady. The lady's next-door neighbours were alerted to the antics of this lot!" exclaimed the headmaster, waving his hand around to indicate the group in question.

Ben kept silent and kept his head down. It seemed that no one knew it was him who had done the alerting. He could do one of two things. He could speak up now and let everyone know that he was the, so say, informant, or he could say nothing and be blamed along with the boys. He was sort of guilty. He had gone along with it to a certain degree and he didn't want to be labelled by the other pupils as being a grass, someone who couldn't be trusted and who went running to adults to tell tales. He looked up and caught his mum's eye. She looked so hurt that a child of hers could act in such a way.

The headmaster continued. "The next-door neighbours, having confronted the boys, who then ran away, were uncertain what to do. Should they call the police? Seemed a bit extreme, but then they realised they knew one of the boys as Jamie Morton and that they had once seen him wearing a Hinchingbrooke School uniform so they contacted me last night. I rang Jamie's house and he was very quick to tell me the names of the others who belonged to this delightful little club. And here we are," he said, finishing with a glare at the boys.

The silence in the room was heavy. No one spoke. The boys kept their heads down. The mention of the police had filled them with dread. Their parents shifted uneasily in their seats, unsure whether to try to defend their offspring or to let them face whatever punishment was coming.

"And, as if things aren't bad enough, Mrs Abelman, the elderly lady in question, is missing!" continued the headmaster. "No one has seen her. She didn't answer her door last night. The neighbours asked around and found out that your mum, Ben, has a key to her house. A key given to her by the family of Mrs Muriel Smith, who used to live next door to you and who is a good friend of Mrs Abelman's and who was the custodian of Mrs Abelman's key before she went into the care home. This morning, the neighbours unlocked Mrs Abelman's front door and went in. Mrs Abelman, it would seem, has left her house at short notice. What do you boys know about this?"

All the boys looked up at this question. Jamie, Ben noticed, wore a worried expression. "I don't know anything about her missing," he said. "I've only seen her that one time, when she came out to tell me off. She's never appeared since. I just assumed she was too scared."

"Too scared!" exclaimed Mary, unable to contain herself any longer. "You bunch of bullies. I'm disgusted.

Disgusted with all of you," and her gaze finished up resting on her son. Ben squirmed in his seat.

"Never appeared since?" questioned the headmaster. "This has been going for a while, hasn't it? It's not a one-off case. You have been systematically targeting this lady over a period of time, haven't you!"

Jamie nodded, looking very sorry for himself.

The telephone on the headmaster's desk rang. He picked up the receiver and listened. "I see. Well thank you for letting me know. This does rather take us in a certain direction," he said to the person on the other end. He put the receiver down.

"Mrs Abelman's neighbours have decided to contact the police and report her as missing. They are worried about her. So, boys, I'm afraid the police are going to be involved after all. Having thought all of this through, I have decided to suspend all of you from school for one week. I will inform your teachers and they can prepare you some work to do from home. This way you can be easily available when the police want to interview you. During your suspension, I want you to think over your actions. This is not the sort of behaviour which befits a pupil of this school and unless I see some proper remorse from you, I may seek to expel you from this school. You are dismissed."

It was playtime at Warburton Church of England Primary School, and Nicola spent it hiding in the toilets. She was in the top year, year six, and she would be following her brother and sister to Hinchingbrooke School the following September. She was very uneasy about this. It was one thing being in the top year. It was an entirely different prospect being reduced to the youngest year of a school. To make matters worse, her two best friends, Lucy and Stephanie, had decided they no longer wanted her around. They had both recently started their periods, a little on the young side perhaps, but they brandished it like a trophy and considered themselves to be women. They didn't want a silly baby like Nicola, who hadn't started her periods, and, from the look of her undeveloped chest, was still a long way off getting them, and who still played with Barbie dolls, hanging around. They had 'woman' things to talk about, such as what kind of menstrual pads were best, and Nicola could not join in.

It wasn't just that they were leaving her out. They made fun of her and wrote little snide comments about some of her photos on Facebook. They remarked on her lack of boobs and suggested that she take some fat off of her thighs, buy a bra and put the fat in the cups. Nicola had never before entertained the thought that she may have fat thighs. No one, not even her brother Ben, who liked to torment and tease her, had ever mentioned her thighs. The result was that she felt very self-conscious. When it came to PE, a subject that used to be one of her favourites, she now couldn't face wearing her PE shorts. She had devised a method of skipping PE by leaning on her mum to write a note of excuse because she had a tummy ache or some other slight ailment, but today she had forgotten to ask for a note. Just as well, really, because her mum was beginning to be suspicious about all of these sudden ailments. Nicola had always been a very healthy individual. Nicola knew, if she wasn't careful, that there would be a trip to the doctors and she didn't want that as there was nothing wrong with her, certainly not in a physical sense. The health of her mind, however, was a different matter. She was beginning to find the idea of food repulsive. Every time her meal was put in front of her, she could feel her, so called, fat thighs getting bigger. She no longer ate her lunch. She used to have school dinners, but she told her mum that she wanted to take a packed lunch instead. It was easier to hide the fact from the dinner ladies that she wasn't eating her sandwiches rather than to not eat a plate of dinner which was on show. The dinner ladies never checked whether she had eaten her packed lunch anyway.

The bell rang, sounding the end of playtime and a return to lessons. Nicola slipped out of the toilets and went to her classroom. PE was the next activity. She had decided she would wear her jogging bottoms and say she had forgotten to bring her shorts.

Ben and his parents had returned home. He was immediately sent to his room to begin his work. "Don't think you are on a week's holiday, my lad!" his dad had shouted before he left for work. His mum said nothing at all. She was too upset.

It wasn't until lunch time that she went up to Ben's room to say she had made a sandwich and he had better come down for it. She couldn't help but notice her son's puffy eyes. He had been crying for most of the morning and a little bit of her heart went out to him.

They ate their food in silence. Mary felt it was too soon to start demanding answers. Let things calm down a little first. When Ben had finished eating, or rather, when he had finished tearing the bread into little balls, his face a reflection of his inner demons, she told him to go out into the garden for a breath of fresh air before returning to his schoolwork.

Outside, Ben mooched around, kicking pebbles, with his hands in his pockets. He had stopped crying. He had no more tears left and his head ached. Whilst mooching, he reflected on his handling of the whole situation. He should have stood up and said something from the very beginning. He should have done ever so many things right from the start. He had handled things badly. He kept saying this in his mind, over and over, like a mantra. Gradually, however, another sound penetrated his thoughts. The sound of sobbing. At first he thought it was his mum, crying in the kitchen, but a quick glance showed him that she was quietly leafing through a magazine while sitting at the table and sipping a cup of tea. He could still hear the sobbing and he stopped scuffing around and listened. It was coming from next door.

No one lives there, thought Ben. He crept up to the high wooden fence and put his eye to a hole which was conveniently located at the right height. At first he could see nothing, but then his eye accustomed itself to squinting through a tiny space. The garden was overgrown with grass almost waist high. His eyeball continued to swivel around and then he saw a woman. She was sitting on some stone steps in the garden, clasping her knees and rocking backwards and forwards. Ben wasted no time. He went back into his house and asked his mum to come and have a look. She came out and peered through the hole.

"Why, it's Mrs Abelman! You know, the lady who is missing!" she exclaimed.

She and Ben quickly went round to next door and into the back garden. Mrs Abelman, on hearing their arrival, looked up in fright and seemed to shrink into herself. She was obviously feeling very vulnerable. There was a streak of what looked like dried blood on her face.

"Mrs Abelman!" said Mary, gently sitting down next to her on the step. "Everyone is very worried about you. The police are looking for you!"

"They are?" asked Esther. "I'm too scared to go home. I thought we were safe but it's started again. Pogroms! That Mr Hitler has a lot to answer for, stirring up such hate!" She continued to rock backwards and forwards in a very agitated state.

Ben frowned. What was she going on about? Hitler? He was long gone!

"There, there," comforted Mary, putting her arm around Esther's shoulders and drawing her close. "It's okay. You are confused. And cold too! You need a hot drink and some food. Come home with us and I can let people know you are safe." Mary stood up, gently pulling Esther to her feet as she did so.

As she slowly got up, Esther's gaze rested squarely on Ben. She blinked and hesitated. "Are you with the Hitler Youth, young man?" Wide-eyed, Ben shook his head.

"It's okay, Mrs Abelman, Hitler and that dreadful time has been over for many years. You have somehow confused the present day with the past. Some warm food will help you to remember," reiterated Mary.

Together they went back to their house and into the warm kitchen. Mary told Ben to put the kettle on and to open a can of tomato soup while she busied herself by ringing the police to inform them that Mrs Abelman had been found and could someone from Social Services, or whichever relevant department they felt appropriate, pay a visit, please?

Abi arrived home that evening, along with Ricky. She had heard some sort of rumour at school to the effect that her brother had been suspended and she was in a state of shock and keen to find out more. Mary took her to one side and explained everything that had happened, including finding Mrs Abelman next door.

"Can we keep this among ourselves, just for tonight at least?" asked Mary, nodding towards the lounge, where Ricky had gone to sit down and wait for Abi. "Who is he, anyway?"

"That's Ricky. He's a boy in my form at school. We've been friends, sort of, for a while. He helped me with the Halloween party last night. You don't mind him coming here at such short notice, do you? Can he stay for tea, if it's okay with his mum?" asked Abi.

"Okay by me. We have one extra already. Mrs Abelman is still here and is staying for the night. She was very confused earlier, mixing the past and present, but she seems to have calmed down and to be more coherent now."

Abi popped her head around the lounge door and beckoned to Ricky. Mrs Abelman was also in the lounge, sitting on the sofa and leafing through a magazine. She was a striking woman with a luxurious head of silver hair. Ricky got up and followed Abi up to her room. She opened the door and told him to go in, then she walked across the landing and put her head round Ben's door. He was sitting at his desk, working from his books. He looked up. Abi was struck by his pale complexion.

"I'm busy at the moment, but we can have a chat later if you like?" she suggested. Ben nodded.

Back in her room, she found Ricky looking at the journal. He was carefully turning the pages. Abi held her breath. What would he say about its condition?

"This is interesting! I've been reading some of it. Do you think it's written by *the* Abigail Williams as in *The*

Crucible's Abigail Williams?" he looked up at Abi as he spoke.

"You can read it!" she exclaimed. "You don't think it's illegible and ready for the scrap heap!"

Ricky looked perplexed. "Well, it's not in the best of condition, but I can certainly read it even though it's a bit difficult to understand the fancy style of writing and weird English and spelling. It's not too bad once you get used to it."

Abi could have kissed him, she was that happy. She had begun to wonder whether she was seeing things, but here was good old Ricky and he also thought the journal was readable. Who would have thought it! Ricky Morris!

There was a knock on the door, and Mary popped her head round. "Only me!" she said, coming fully into the room. "I've brought this back," she continued, brandishing the tear-shaped vase. "I had put some scented dried flowers in it, but, for some strange reason, they went slimy, so I took it away, cleaned it up and now I'm bringing it back. I think it's best to leave it empty. It's very pretty on its own."

She placed the vase back on the windowsill and turned to smile at Ricky. "Hello, I'm Abi's mum," she said, a little needlessly, as Ricky had already worked that out. She offered her hand and he shook it. "Tea is almost ready. I hope you like cottage pie?" Ricky nodded. "Good. Well you had both better come downstairs then. Abi, you can set the table for me, please."

Mary stood by the open bedroom door and impatiently waved them out of the room. Abi was surprised by her mother's attitude. She didn't normally come bustling into her bedroom with a contrived reason when Abi had some friends visiting. She frowned and then a thought crept into her mind. *It's because my friends have always been girls. She was worried we were up to something!* Abi felt herself blush as she walked past her mother. Ricky, thank goodness, didn't seem to think there was anything unusual going on.

The meal that night was an unusual one. For a start, there were two new faces at the table, which altered the family atmosphere. Secondly, there was the trouble with Ben and thirdly, Nicola, normally a quick eater, was idly shovelling her food around her plate, but not actually eating anything. Mary kept watching her with a little worried frown creasing her brow.

Mrs Abelman hadn't had much to say. She had said please and thank you when she had to, but, otherwise, she had been quiet. She finished her helping of cottage pie, which she had eaten with relish, having not had a substantial hot meal in the last forty-eight hours, and placed her knife and fork neatly together on the plate and looked around her.

"It's very nice, the changes you have made to the cottage," she said. "Jean would have approved."

"Ah yes!" exclaimed Robert. "You knew my grandmother, didn't you!"

Esther nodded. "She was a good friend of mine. Her, and Muriel, who lived next door. We shared in each other's lives for quite a few years. Had a lot of laughs and some heartache, too." She turned to look at Ricky. "I see, from your uniform, that you are a pupil at Hinchingbrooke. Jean always reckoned that the old house there used to belong to her ancestors a long time ago. Do you know anything about that claim?" she asked, turning her attention back to Robert.

"There is some rumour in our family that that is the case, although nothing has ever been proved – not that anyone in the family has tried to find any evidence, mind you. Wouldn't know where to start anyway," answered Robert.

"Dad!" exclaimed Abi. "You've never said! I've been going to that school for a few years now and I had no idea that the old house used to belong to our family!"

"Steady on, Abi! It's only a rumour. Don't go getting too excited!" said Robert in a cautionary tone. "Perhaps we could look into it, just for our own interest, like. We don't want to start yelling it from the rooftops. Besides, who but us would be interested anyway?"

"I don't know, it's pretty amazing, if your ancestors did own it. Does that mean you are descendants of Oliver Cromwell, then?" asked Ricky.

"Well, I suppose so," said Robert, rubbing his chin in reflection. "I'm ashamed to say that I don't know the history of the old Hinchingbrooke House. When did it become part of a school, for instance? Was it always the home of the Cromwells? If so, then it must be that they were our ancestors."

They all thought about that for a minute or two and then Mary decided to change the subject. "I saw some newts in our pond today," she said, winking.

Robert looked surprised. "Already? Didn't take them long to move in did it?" He laughed.

"Pond?" asked Esther

"Yes. We've put a pond in the garden. No fish in it – they just pollute. I've always wanted a pond, ever since I was a little boy and now I've got one," answered Robert.

Esther looked down at her hands. They were clutched together in consternation. "Where in the garden is this pond?" she asked, dreading the answer.

"Oh, if you go out of the back door and turn left towards the back gate, it's in an area of the garden that has no trees. Whereas the trees would have shaded the pond in summer, I didn't want them dropping all their leaves in it in autumn, so that treeless area of the garden seemed the best place," explained Robert.

Esther placed her elbows on the table and put her head in her hands and moaned.

Her fellow diners watched her with concern on their faces. What was wrong with her? Mary worried that she was becoming confused again, but what had caused it?

Esther lifted her head and looked at the family. Maybe they hadn't dug in the right area after all. Dare she ask?

"Tell me, did you find anything when you dug down a way into the soil?"

"Oh yes!" it was Nicola who spoke. "We found a trunk with a wooden doll, a book and a vase in it."

There was silence. Esther looked worried. *No*, thought Abi, *it's worse than that. She looks frightened.*

Esther let out a jagged sigh. "What have you done?"

Chapter Five

Everyone was silent. What did Mrs Abelman mean?

Esther was quiet. She hadn't meant to blurt out that question. She couldn't tell them the truth, because the truth was too fantastic. They wouldn't believe her and would think she had lost her mind. She would have to think of something though, because they weren't about to let a comment like that pass by unchallenged.

"What do you mean, Mrs Abelman?" asked Abi. She was remembering Michelle's idea that maybe the three old ladies knew something about the trunk buried in their garden.

"Oh, I only meant that Jean wouldn't have approved. She liked her garden just the way it was. She would have thought a pond was a waste of time and money," explained Esther, knowing that her explanation was a little on the lame side, but it was the best she could do.

"You are probably right," agreed Robert. "Grandma didn't take kindly to change. But it's our garden now and I think she would be happy that at least it is family who are still living in her cottage, rather than strangers."

"Oh, I completely agree," answered Esther, relieved that her explanation had been accepted. She glanced at Abi and then checked her relief. Abi looked like she knew that Esther wasn't being honest with them. She secretly prayed that the girl would leave off asking any more questions.

Mary pushed her chair back and began collecting together the dinner plates. Ricky helped her to do this, much to Abi's surprise. She was beginning to realise that maybe she had underestimated him. Fortunately for Esther, Abi's thoughts were now directed towards Ricky and any further questions she had been about to ask were put on hold – for the time being. For dessert there was fresh rhubarb crumble, made with big, crunchy red stalks the size of cricket bats, which were growing wild in the garden. Everyone enjoyed it and scraped their pudding bowls clean.

After the meal, Ben went back to his room. He didn't have to, as the school day was over, but he felt safer in his bedroom. He didn't want to spend time in Mrs Abelman's company as he felt guilty and ashamed. Nothing had been said to her about his involvement in her persecution, although she was aware that the boys responsible for her victimisation had been identified and punished. Ben knew he should apologise to her but he just couldn't face doing this at the moment. He needed to form his apology in his head first, before he faced Mrs Abelman.

Nicola had managed not to eat too much of the cottage pie, but had failed miserably over the rhubarb crumble. This was her favourite dessert and she had eaten it up hungrily.

Her mother had been pleased to see an empty bowl for a change. Once Nicola was in her room, she sat on her bed and viewed herself in the long mirror opposite. Her thighs seemed to spread out all over the duvet. She poked and pinched at them in frustration and the crumble she had eaten was sitting very heavily in her stomach. She thought about making herself sick to get rid of it but she had a fear of being sick and so she did not adopt this approach. She would just have to make up for her over-indulgence tomorrow. Instead, she went to her wardrobe and pulled out her Barbie doll. Her friends liked to accuse her of still playing with dolls, but this wasn't strictly true as Nicola liked to design and make dolls' clothes. She often picked apart old clothes so that she could re-use them for material and drew out clothes patterns and then cut out the material. She sewed the clothes by hand and her stitches were very neat. Her mum thought she was very talented.

Nicola picked up her sketch pad and pencil and began to draw an idea for a new dress for Barbie. At least she could lose herself in this activity and she was able to forget about the spiteful comments she was constantly receiving from her friends.

Downstairs, Mary was busily making preparations for Esther to sleep the night. The study doubled as a spare guest bedroom and it had a sofa-bed in it. Mary pulled out the frame and unfolded mattress from under the seat cushions and locked the legs in place. Next she made up the bed with fresh sheets, plumping up the pillows and placing the sofa seat cushions as a headboard. Pleased with her efforts, she quickly dusted off the computer, then the desk and then stood a mirror on it. She popped some clean towels on the end of the bed and pulled the curtains, ready for the night.

Abi and Ricky had gone down the garden to the shed after the meal. Abi hadn't like to take him back up to her room, after her mother's reaction previously and Mrs Abelman was sitting in the lounge along with Robert, watching television, and so the shed was the next best place which would allow them to talk without being overheard.

It was dark in the shed and Abi quickly switched on the large torches which she had used to create the eerie glow for the Halloween party. The beam from the torches picked out what looked like spots of blood on the shed floor. Abi frowned. Maybe one of the girls had hurt herself as they made their hasty escape from fear last night.

Ricky and Abi sat on the bean bags and Abi told Ricky all about the strange happenings which had occurred since the trunk had been dug up. Ricky was interested.

"I think the key to it is to try to find out where the doll and other stuff came from," he said. "I think that Mrs Abelman knows something. I didn't buy the excuse she gave your dad, did you?"

"No, I didn't either," said Abi, shaking her head. "I don't want to push her though. She's been through enough

recently. I might get the chance to ask her sometime."
Despite her mum having asked if they could keep Mrs
Abelman's story to themselves for the time being, Abi
found herself telling Ricky about the little gang of bullies
and how they, including her brother, had been suspended
from school for a week. Ricky said he had heard about the
suspension, but not about the reason for it. He asked if this
kind of behaviour was out of character for her brother.

"Oh yes, definitely!" exclaimed Abi, vehemently.
"He's normally a very nice person, though I hate admitting
it!" Ricky grinned. He had a younger brother also and it
didn't do for the older sibling to show any signs of
admiration for the younger. There was too much at stake
and the younger sibling had to know their place.

Later that evening, Abi was getting ready for bed. As usual
she was sitting at her dressing table, removing her make-
up. Just recently, there hadn't been any more funny noises
at night and she had almost begun to think that there was a
rational explanation for them, or that maybe the noises and
whispering had been a product of her imagination.

After Ricky had left for home, Abi had paid a visit to
Ben in his bedroom. She asked him for his side of the story.
Ben felt encouraged that at last, someone, even if it was
only his sister, was interested enough to question him
about his role in the Mrs Abelman affair. For a minute he
toyed with the problem of whether to tell her the whole
truth. He decided he would, if only to have someone on his

side for once. He could swear her to secrecy and so he told her how he had been against the idea of tormenting Mrs Abelman and how he and Jamie had fallen out over it. Then he explained how he had alerted Mrs Abelman's neighbours to the fact that there was a group of boys throwing eggs at her windows, by banging on their front door and ringing their doorbell.

"Oh, Ben! You must let Mum and Dad know all of this. You did the right thing and you shouldn't be suspended! exclaimed Abi.

Ben shook his head. "For some reason Jamie hasn't realised that it was me who got the neighbours' attention. I think he thinks I just went home. He certainly hasn't given me any evils over it anyway. I don't want to be seen as a tell-tale. I won't have any friends if this gets out, so I want you to promise, Abi, not to say anything to Mum and Dad. I can do a week's suspension and then slowly mend my reputation. After a while it will all be forgotten about."

"But Mum and Dad are so disappointed in you. They think they haven't been good parents. You need to let them know that you are the person they have always believed you to be. Perhaps you can tell them in the same way you have told me?"

Again Ben shook his head. "No. They will want to let the school know and I don't want that."

"Then I shall tell them. It's not right that you should be punished!"

"Abi!" Ben's voice had a warning tone to it. "I've told you this in confidence. Please don't go meddling."

Abi looked at her brother with a frustrated expression on her face. "Okay," she mumbled. Secretly she would try to find a way to convey to her parents the quandary Ben was in. She ruffled the top of Ben's head and left him to it, quietly closing his bedroom door as she left.

Now, as she brushed her hair, her thoughts turned to Ricky. He was a lot more mature when he wasn't with his friends. Abi found she quite liked him. She went off into a trance, the rhythm of her own hair brushing relaxing her and making her feel nicely tired. Suddenly, there was a movement behind her, a sort of change of light which she caught in the reflection of the mirror. Surprised, she turned around to see who had come into her room. There was no one there. She shrugged and turned back. She looked into the mirror. The face looking back at her wasn't her reflection! Abi jumped up and let out a cry of alarm. She carried on backing back. The door behind her opened and Ben put his head round.

"Everything all right?" he asked, a concerned frown creased between his eyes.

Abi pointed to the mirror. "There. There's something in the mirror... a face... not mine!"

Ben looked to where his sister was pointing. The reflection in the mirror was quite normal, highlighting its view of the bedroom.

Abi risked looking. "It's gone. There was a girl looking back at me. Honest!"

"Well, everything's back to normal now. It will have been a trick of light. It can't be anything else," said Ben reassuringly.

Abi, although still shaken, had to agree. Ben could see she was going to be all right, so he closed her door and went back to his own room. Abi finished getting ready for bed and decided she would leave her lamp on overnight. She hadn't done this for a few nights.

Nicola was having a strange dream. She was in the woods at the back of her house. She could still see the house, with its welcoming lights, but at the same time it seemed a long way away. When she tried to walk to it, she found that she couldn't. There seemed to be an invisible wall between her and it. She was only wearing her nightie and had nothing on her feet, yet she wasn't cold and the rough, twiggy ground didn't hurt her feet. She wasn't alone. There was a girl with her. The girl looked like Nicola, but was dressed in the fashion of a bygone era and she carried a book which she brandished towards Nicola.

"Go on, sign it," she demanded, proffering a feathered quill. "Sign the book and those girls who are making your life a misery will suffer. Don't you want to get your own back on them?"

Nicola shook her head. She turned instead to go home. Immediately the girl was in front of her.

"If you don't sign it, it will be the worse for you!" she hissed.

Nicola pushed past her. There was nothing to push. The girl vaporised and appeared again sitting on one of the branches of a tree. Nicola kept running. Her feet were so very heavy and the house seemed to get further and further away. "Mum!" she screamed over and over, all the while fighting against the branches as they caught and held onto her nightie and tangled with her hair.

Suddenly, there was light. Her mum was at the side of her bed, gently smoothing her forehead and saying everything was all right, that it was only a nightmare. Slowly, Nicola's breathing returned to normal and her heart slowed to an acceptable beat.

"Get out of bed a minute, Nick, while I remake it. You've got the covers in a right tangle!" said Mary. She deftly shook out the duvet and tucked the base sheet back under the mattress and plumped up the pillow. This done, she invited Nicola to get back in. "Can I get you some warm milk to settle you?" she asked.

Nicola shook her head. "I'll be okay now, Mum, thank you. I just need to get back to sleep," she stated, smiling wanly at her mother.

After her mum had gone, sleep didn't return for a while. Nicola lay there, trying to visualise what she had been dreaming about. It was all too shady for her to remember. She turned on to her side and gradually her eyes closed.

The following morning, as she got out of bed and placed her feet on the bedside rug, she was surprised to find that they hurt, and she had a scratch on one of her ankles. She couldn't remember how she had managed to get such a scratch. She sat on the edge of the bed and tried to retrace her movements from the day before. There was nothing that she had done which could account for her scratch and sore feet. She was puzzled, and yet there was something at the back of her mind, a fleeting memory, which was gone as soon as she tried to analyse it. She shrugged her shoulders and decided to get ready for school, hurrying off to the bathroom then getting dressed in record time.

Ben finished scraping his spoon around his bowl. He had just finished a big serving of porridge. He put the bowl to one side and selected a piece of toast from the toast rack. As he lavishly spread marmalade on it, he allowed himself a secret glance at Mrs Abelman. There was only the two of them sitting at the table, finishing off their breakfast. Everyone else had been and gone and his mum was upstairs, sorting out a washing load from the linen basket. Ben thought it might be a good time to make his apology to Mrs Abelman.

"I'm sorry, Mrs Abelman, but I was one of the gang who visited your garden on Halloween," he said, swallowing his mouthful of toast. It seemed to stick part way down his throat.

Esther looked across at him. "I've only seen the one boy skulking about in my garden and yelling through my letterbox – the boy I told off a couple of weeks ago and who has been plaguing me ever since."

Ben nodded. "Yes, but on Halloween, he had persuaded the rest of us to join in and I was one of them. I'm sorry. We shouldn't have done it. I knew it was wrong, but I still went along with it."

Esther regarded him for a minute. She was feeling weary. The last couple of weeks had taken it out of her. She hadn't been sleeping very well and last night was no exception. The bed in the study had been comfortable enough but her thoughts kept her awake. Someone from Social Services was supposed to be visiting her this morning, at ten o'clock, at her own home, so they could see and assess her current style of living and she was all worked up and wondering what new lifestyle they would want her to adopt. "I've had a chat with one of my neighbours, you know, over the phone. They tell me that there were three boys running amok and chucking eggs around in my garden. So, were you one of these?" asked Esther, looking across at Ben.

Ben shook his head. "No, I had decided to go home before we were caught," he explained.

"So, you were the boy who furiously rang the doorbell of my neighbour's house then," stated Esther. "Another neighbour was out walking her dog that night and witnessed a young boy leave my front garden and go to the next house where he rang the bell and banged on the door and then ran and hid in the bushes across the road. At first she thought it was all part of the Halloween rubbish but then, as she watched the other boys getting caught, she realised that the boy in the bushes, who had crept away as soon as my neighbour was on the case, was merely trying to get help. That boy was you, wasn't it?" she asked.

Ben nodded.

"So why have you been suspended? Didn't you explain all this to your headmaster and your parents?

"I didn't because I don't want to be seen as an informer. I'll have no friends and anyway, I'm not completely innocent, I was part of it at the beginning. It just felt all wrong though and so I did what I could to put a stop to it without placing the spotlight on me," explained Ben.

"I wish you had told us that, Ben," said his mum from the doorway. She had overheard the conversation.

Ben shut his eyes in frustration. Now there would be phone calls to the school, demanding that he be taken off suspension and his life would disappear down the loo as a result.

Mary came and sat down at the table. "I do understand why you want to keep quiet about this," she said. "If you need to continue with your suspension to save face in front of your friends, then I suppose this is what we will do. I'll have to run it past your dad first though. But you will have to continue with your schoolwork – there will be no slacking!"

Ben hugged his mum. He was grateful that she understood. He only hoped that his dad also understood.

As it was nearing ten o'clock, the time of Esther's appointment with Social Services, Mary asked if Ben would help to carry some of Esther's belongings, her makeshift bedding, for example, which she had left her house with when she had expected to be sleeping in the shed.

Together the three of them set off for Esther's house. They let themselves in through the front door and Esther immediately turned up the thermostat on her heating to dispel the chill which pervaded the house. The ground floor windows at the back of the house were still smeared with egg.

The meeting with Rachel, as she introduced herself, from Social Services, went quite well. Esther was relieved that it was decided that she could still cope with living by herself. The state of the garden was raised, however, and it was suggested that maybe she should hire a gardener. This was something she would have to pay for herself as she had the means to do so. At this suggestion, Esther merely nodded and said she would look into it. Ben smiled to himself. He could tell that she wouldn't be paying out for a gardener and so after Rachel had left, he put voice to an idea he had had.

"I can do your gardening for you if you like," he said.

Esther looked at him and then at his mother. Mary was looking at Ben, a look of surprise on her face.

"I don't mind," continued Ben.

"Well, if it's okay with your parents, young man, then that would be lovely!" exclaimed Esther.

Before they left, Ben and Mary wiped the back windows clean. The upstairs windows had escaped the aim of the boys and so, with it being only the lower ground windows, the task was soon completed.

Today had been an okay day, thought Nicola, as she walked home from school. Lucy had been off sick and Stephanie had spent the day hanging out with Nicola, rather like they used to before things had turned sour. Nicola found herself forgiving Stephanie for all of the hurtful comments which had been made. She also harboured a wish that Lucy took a while to get better, but then felt dreadful for thinking it. However, she was finding out that three was a crowd and she was tired of being the odd one out. It felt nice to be in a twosome. Today, Stephanie had been a ready partner for her in PE and a few other lessons, instead of the teacher having to find one for her.

Just before she reached home, Nicola threw away her packed lunch in the waste bin by the village shop.

Chapter six

Abi had been reading *In the Devil's Snare* and was finding it quite difficult. She realised this was because she had hardly any knowledge of the history of the first settlers to arrive on the shores of the new world, or the United States, as it later became known. The King Philip Wars and King William Wars were talked about a good deal. But who on earth were King Philip and King William? She had researched online names of history books which might help and had found and ordered, through her trusty account with AbeBooks, a book entitled *The Mayflower and the Pilgrims' New World* by Nathaniel Philbrick and it was proving to be very good in helping her to understand some of the history. The early settlers, it seemed, had been on very good terms with the Native Americans, who had taught the settlers how to grow crops and how to preserve the food so it could be used throughout the harsh winter months. They had even sold some of their land to the settlers. The settlers, in turn, had managed to convert a good many of the natives to Christianity and the natives had taken Christian names. Such was the bonhomie which had existed between the two civilisations. So, King Philip and King William were Native Americans who had adopted Christian names and who had eventually waged war on the settlers when wrongdoings and mistrust had built up on both sides. It was necessary, Abi felt, to have a sound knowledge of the kind of trials and tribulations the settlers in Salem Village had had to endure. The more she read about the subject, the more she understood the point the author of *In the Devil's Snare* was making. The New England communities had been living in fear for a great number of years. Fear of attack by the natives, fear of illness and fear of each other.

Alongside reading of the text books, she was also reading *Abigail's* journal. After *Abigail* and her family had arrived at the farm where they were to help out with the daily chores, life had settled down to a routine. The work was hard and *Abigail* would tumble into her bed on an evening exhausted from the day's toils. To Abi, it seemed a tough existence of all work and no play. The family would rise at the crack of dawn, work all day and then the evenings were spent reading from the Bible. Puritan children were taught to read and write so that they could then read the Scriptures for themselves.

Abi thought the life harsh. Surely all work and no play would have given rise to a grim view of the world? Wouldn't it have made people look sternly upon those who it was considered were being frivolous with their time? Wouldn't this attitude help to spread a judgemental atmosphere? And, amidst all of this, a group of girls somehow managed to gain credibility in their accusations of seeing witches on every street corner, so as to speak.

Rather like the Americans, who in the 1950s, reckoned there were Russian spies everywhere, which was the parallel Arthur Miller was keen to draw attention to when he wrote *The Crucible*.

These were the questions which Abi was posing to herself as she picked up the journal to read for a while, before settling down to sleep.

April 1689

At last the weather is getting warmer and most of the snow has now melted. The land will need tilling and the crops will need planting. There is plenty of work to be done. You would think that the prospect of longer, warmer days would bring some sort of jovial atmosphere to our lives. Not so. During the winter months, hostilities between native and settler are put to one side and the battle to survive the perishing cold takes precedence. With the warmer weather, we are out and about, mending fences, sowing seeds, and collecting eggs and therefore extremely vulnerable. There is a tension in the air thick enough to interfere with breathing. I have noticed my ribs constantly ache because my breathing is shallow, and this makes me feel lightheaded. Worryingly, there have been reports of a farm having been attacked, its owners mercilessly killed and the homestead set alight. Just the other day, two farmhands were attacked whilst checking on some cows in one of their fields. Consequently we are all on edge.

If it wasn't for the fear of attack, my life would feel dreary indeed. Six out of the seven days are all the same and the seventh is equally as tedious; worship and reading from the Scriptures. I feel as though I want something more from life. I can read and I can write and I have a thirst for knowledge. I have no interest in making quilts from bits of old clothes or for instruction in any of the duties considered necessary for a girl to learn so that she will make a good wife. I feel at odds with my mother and my father is disappointed in me. I am argumentative and am constantly told that I should know my place. It is the role of good Puritan girls to be subservient, but I cannot bring myself to act in this way.

The other day, Uncle Samuel came up from Boston to pay us a visit to see how we are getting along. I am not keen on him. He has his eye on being the Reverend in Salem Village. He has come late to the ministry, having first been in charge of his family's plantation in Barbados and then a business man. I do not feel he has been called by God to deliver the message. His pious air is of an artificial nature and his desire to be a man of God has more to do with vanity than it is with showing any compassion.

I shiver with doom when I think of him taking the worship at the village and I hope he is not offered the position.

Abi glanced at her clock and decided it was time to get some shut eye. She placed the journal on her bedside cabinet and clicked off her light. So, she thought, *Abigail* had had a sort of premonition of the tragedy to come. She didn't like Samuel Parris and she had admitted that the whole community was tense and scared of attack. It was as though *Abigail* was setting the scene.

As yet, Abi hadn't put pen to paper regarding her English homework and her ideas for the new play. Her teacher had been a little surprised by what seemed to be a lack of effort on Abi's part. Normally Abi was at the forefront when it came to creative writing. She had had to explain to her teacher how she was doing a lot of reading and research first before she put her ideas down on paper and listed the titles of the books she had purchased. She did divulge the idea that the communities up and down New England were suffering from a great fear and that this had somehow played its part in the tragedy of the witch crisis of 1692 and that she was trying to think of a way to arrive at a new concept for the play. Her teacher had been supportive but had explained that she really needed something in writing to be able to show to the Drama department.

Abi sighed and rolled over in bed. She was now looking in the direction of the window. Her curtains, of a lightweight material, were drawn. They did not completely blank out the light cast by the moon and so she was not immediately concerned by the curious glow which was emitting from behind the drapes. Indeed, it took her a while to realise that the glow could not be from the moon as the moon was not out tonight and anyway, the light was too low to be the moon. It seemed to hover just above the level of the windowsill. She frowned. *What on earth could be causing that?* she thought. Loathe to get out of bed and lose the warmth she had built up under the covers, she lay there thinking. The only object on the sill was the vase. As she watched, the glow became even more luminous, until she could bear the mystery no longer.

She threw back her bedcovers and bounded over to the window, swishing back the curtains with a vengeance. A shock was waiting for her. The vase was filled with a bright, creamy mist. It swirled around in the bulbous bowl of the vase. Abi stared, transfixed. Her first thought was that it reminded her of a genie in a bottle and she almost expected the mist to collect into the shape of a man and make its way out of its prison, rather like the genie in Aladdin, or in other fairytales.

As she watched, she was aware of a slight noise, a kind of a whisper, coming from the vase. She drew nearer, and after a little hesitation, put her ear over the top of the neck of the vase, as though she was listening to a conch shell, which always seemed to echo the noise of the sea. The sound from the vase was an indistinguishable whisper. She couldn't make out any words but she had the feeling of being gently sucked into a vortex, as though whatever was in the glass was trying to pull her in. She tried to lift her head away, but it was too heavy to move. She felt as though some stronger will was taking over hers. Then, just as she almost succumbed to whatever the glass had in store for her, someone started smoothing her hair and humming and began to pull her head up from the vase and to lead her back to bed. Abi was terrified. As far as she could tell, there was no one there, yet the gentle stroking of her hair continued after she was back in her bed with the covers tucked up around her, covers she was sure she had not pulled up herself. Her eyes became heavy, despite her terror, and she began to feel sleepy. Just before she gave in to sleep, she noticed that *Peg* was missing from her home on the wall.

Nicola was feeling very sad and unsettled. Lucy was back at school, although she still didn't look well, and Stephanie had immediately dropped Nicola in favour of Lucy. Every minute they were together they seemed to look in her direction and then whisper something in each other's ear and giggle. Somehow, after the day before, when Stephanie had been really friendly and their relationship was, apparently, back on track, today's betrayal was more hurtful than ever. Also, as if things weren't bad enough, her teacher, Miss Broad, had informed Nicola that she was to stay behind after school, as she wished to have a talk with both Nicola and her mum. Apparently, Miss Broad had telephoned her mum earlier that morning asking if today after school was a convenient time for her to pop in for a chat. Nicola had no idea what this chat was to be about and Miss Broad's facial expression gave nothing away – except that she didn't seem annoyed or cross with her. So it was a mystery.

Ben had worked like a traction engine all morning in his room. He had done a whole school day's worth of work in half a day so that he could go over to Mrs Abelman's house and begin working on her garden. He was immensely looking forward to this, which surprised him. His father had given his consent about doing the gardening and, after much diplomatic persuasion by his mum, had also finally understood why Ben wanted to remain suspended. As long as Ben kept up with the homework he had been set, then a bit of hard work, digging and pulling up weeds, would do him good.

After his lunch, Ben put on some older clothes and a dilapidated pair of trainers he found in the bottom of his wardrobe. They had a musty, soggy sock kind of odour and he wrinkled his nose in disgust. Still, they would do for gardening in. He didn't want to use his new white, trainers as he would get grass stains on them when he cut the grass.

He set off for the short walk to Mrs Abelman's with a definite spring in his step. He was actually looking forward to helping out with the garden. When Mrs Abelman opened the door to allow him in, he gave her a broad smile.

"I thought I would start with mowing the lawn, both front and back. Do you have a lawn mower?" he asked her.

"Yes, it's in the shed. It's a petrol mower, so you don't, or I don't, need to worry about you running over the cable and electrocuting yourself!" said Esther, dryly. "Have you used one before?"

Ben nodded. He had been known to use the petrol lawnmower at home on occasion, usually when he wanted to earn a bit of extra pocket money. "Who has cut your grass in the past?" he asked.

"I used to mow it myself after my husband died, but then just recently it has become too much for me. My next-door neighbour does it for me occasionally, but he is a busy man and I don't like to keep asking," explained Esther.

He set to work on the back garden. It would take several mowings to get the length down to an acceptable height. It was damp down at root level and this made the task quite difficult. Nevertheless, he persevered. He whistled to himself while he worked. There was a forlorn looking compost heap at the back of the garden and he emptied the grass cuttings onto it. He sniffed the air. He always liked the smell of newly cut grass. It reminded him of summer, even though it was early November. Hopefully the grass wouldn't grow again now until the spring next year.

When he had finished the back garden grass, Mrs Abelman called him in for a drink. She had made a pot of tea. Ben would have preferred some Coke, but she had made a coconut and cherry cake to accompany the tea so Ben just showed his appreciation by sitting down and accepting some cake and sipping the tea out of a bone china cup. It was surprisingly good, both the cake and the tea.

"I like to drink my tea out of a proper teacup," said Esther, watching him enjoy the fruits of her morning's labours. It gave her a warm feeling to see someone tucking into a cake she had made. It had been a long time since someone had appreciated her cooking. "Would you like another piece?"

"Yes, but I'd better not. I won't be able to eat my tea and then I'll have Mum on my back!" said Ben, grinning. "I'm just going to run the mower over the front grass before I head for home."

While he was working on the front garden, he noticed Jamie walking along the pavement. He stopped when he reached Esther's house. Jamie had a big grin on his face and while this annoyed Ben to the extent that he wanted to smack the smile off his face, he was, at the same time, relieved that Jamie appeared none the wiser over how the gang had been discovered.

"All right, mate?" asked Jamie. "Your dad got you doing the old bag's gardening now, has he?"

Ben made a vague noise in his throat and hoped this would pass as an answer.

"Not much longer now and our suspension will be over," Jamie continued. "I've been working on my 'suitably contrite' expression for the benefit of the headmaster. I guess you doing the gardening will also go down well."

Ben nodded. He really had nothing to say to Jamie. He couldn't believe they used to be best friends. Jamie had changed so much – or was it himself who had changed?

Esther was watching the boys from her front window. She could tell from Ben's rigid back that he was feeling uncomfortable at having been found to be doing her gardening. She walked to her front door and opened it. "Ben!" she shouted from her doorstep. "Your dad didn't send you round here so you could waste time talking to your mates!"

Ben looked surprised.

"Jeez, she's a right old cow, that one," whispered Jamie. "I'm off before we get into any more trouble. See you at school on Monday." He patted Ben on the back in a show of camaraderie.

Esther watched him walk away. *He's bad news,* she thought to herself. She turned her attention back to Ben. "I'm sorry if I sounded a little imperialistic just now but it would be best if your friend got the idea that it was your father who has sent you here to do my gardening. It maintains your cover in the whole egg-throwing debacle," she said, grinning.

"Ah," said Ben, a look of understanding crossing his face. "I see! Thanks." Privately he was relieved that Jamie was oblivious to his part in the proceedings.

After school was finished, Nicola remained behind, as requested. She whiled away the time waiting in the classroom for her mum to arrive by studying her handiwork of that afternoon. Miss Broad had asked her to make a display board from the photos which had been taken when the class had gone on a geography field trip to Grafton Water in September, just at the start of the new school term. She had sifted through all of the photos, trying to decide which were the most worthy of making it onto the display board. One picture in particular had caught her attention. It was of Lucy and Stephanie, each pulling some kind of exaggerated fashion model's pose. Nicola had been the photographer on that occasion. Everything had been okay between them then.

Nicola's chin quivered as she now looked at the photo up on the board. Out of the two girls, Lucy and Stephanie, she disliked Lucy the most. She felt that Lucy was the one who was in charge of all the nasty comments and that Stephanie merely followed in her shadow. Now secured on the display board, the photo of the girls looked down on her and their facial expressions, where once they seemed full of fun – fun in which she was involved – now seemed to mock her. On the table next to the display board, the tin of tacks, which she had used earlier, was still there. She picked up one of the tacks and studied it for a moment before pressing it into the middle of the photo, where Lucy's midriff was.

Ha! thought Nicola. *I hope you felt that.*

She could hear Miss Broad and her mother approaching the classroom, so she hurriedly sat down at her desk.

"Ah!" said Miss Broad. "Here she is." She closed the classroom door and indicated for them to pull up a chair each while she sat behind her large desk, situated under the blackboard at the front of the classroom.

"Now, I'll get straight to the point. We are a little worried about your daughter, Mrs Williams. It has been noted by the dinner ladies that Nicola doesn't eat her packed lunch."

"Well, her lunch box is always empty when I take it out of her school bag in the evening," explained Mary, glancing at Nicola for confirmation. Nicola kept her head down, not wanting to meet anybody's eyes.

Miss Broad shook her head. "Apparently she sits at the packed lunch table and goes through the motions, but the dinner ladies are of the opinion that she isn't eating anything."

Mary frowned. "Nicola, what is going on?" she asked.

Nicola didn't answer. The silence seemed to stretch before her, yet there was a roaring in her ears and her cheeks were becoming hot. The lack of food in her stomach was making her feel sick and she could feel a heat collecting around her neck.

"Also," continued the teacher. "There seems to be some issue between Nicola and her two friends, Lucy and Stephanie."

At this, Nicola looked up. How did Miss Broad know that?

"And I'm wondering whether there is a connection between this and the not eating of the lunch? And, Nicola always seems to be finding an excuse not to do PE anymore and, when she does take part, she has taken to wearing her jogging bottoms instead of her shorts."

Mary looked at Nicola. She was beginning to think that she didn't know what was going on with her children's lives anymore. She had always prided herself on being an astute mother, the kind that was always one step ahead of any issues her off spring might have – but what with Ben and now Nicola – it brought into question her parenting.

"Everyone thinks I'm fat," blurted out Nicola, unshed tears pooling in her eyes. The heat surrounding her neck and the pounding in her ears grew worse and when she looked at Miss Broad, she seemed to be floating above her desk and speaking to her from a great distance away.

"Fat!" exclaimed Mary. "Why, there's nothing to you! Whose been saying this? I'd like to know. I'll give them a piece of my mind!" Mary's temper was up and she was ready to tell anyone exactly what she thought of them.

Nicola, unable to say anything, suddenly threw up over the schoolroom floor. There was hardly anything to bring up but her poor stomach, once it had started, couldn't stop the awful retching.

Both mother and teacher rushed to her aid. Miss Broad fetched a glass of water and her mum placed a cool hand over the back of her neck. Gradually Nicola began to feel better.

There was plenty to talk about at the Williams's home that night. As soon as Abi arrived home, her mother took her to one side and told her about Nicola. Abi was incensed.

"Have you noticed anything amiss on Facebook?" asked Mary.

Abi shook her head. "I haven't been on Facebook for such a long time. I'll have a look in a minute," and she disappeared upstairs

Once in her room, Abi threw her heavy bag onto her bed and logged on to Facebook. She had such a lot of notifications but instead of working through these, she went straight to Nicola's page. What she read there made her blood boil.

"Mum, come and have a look at this!" she yelled down the stairs.

"Just look at these comments," she continued, when Mary came into the room and peered over her daughter's shoulder.

"Oh, the spiteful little minxes. They are supposed to be her best friends. Miss Broad definitely has to see this!" exclaimed Mary. "I should have realised something was the matter. She hasn't been eating properly for a while, but I put it down to growing pains."

Nicola popped her head around the door. "You've seen it then?" she stated.

Mary and Abi looked at her.

"Listen," said Abi. "They are just two silly little girls with nothing better to do," she continued, trying to sound reassuring.

"But look at how many laughing face emojis there are! Everyone thinks I have fat thighs and no boobs!"

"For goodness' sake, you're ten years old. Who has boobs at ten years old?" shouted Mary. She was angry and frustrated and felt like banging lots of heads together.

Abi gave her mum's shoulders a squeeze and then ushered her out of the bedroom. "You go and count to ten, or something. I'll have a little talk with Nick," she whispered, closing the door.

She patted the bed, inviting Nicola to come sit on it next to her. She then pulled her smart phone out of her bag and accessed her photos. Scrolling through her collection, she finally came to the one she wanted, tapped on it so it filled the screen and showed Nicola.

"There," said Abi. "Who's this, then?"

Nicola looked at the photo and frowned. It looked like herself but she didn't recognise the shorts being worn. Then it dawned on her. "It's you, Abi, isn't it?"

Abi nodded. "I'm the same age there as you are now. What is your first impression of the photo... and be honest?"

"Well... you look really pretty, which is a bit embarrassing because I thought it was me at first!"

"Exactly! We are so alike, we could be twins separated by five years. You have nothing to be ashamed of and if those so-called friends think there is, then it's their problem, not yours. Own yourself and be proud," said Abi, giving her sister a hug.

Later, everyone was helping to prepare the evening meal. Robert had been told about the online bullying Nicola had had to put up with and he wasn't impressed and hoped that the school would be able to sort it out, otherwise he would be getting involved and he wouldn't be taking any prisoners.

Nicola grinned at her dad's warning as she chopped some carrots. It was nice to know that her family cared. It felt like she had someone on her side at last and she was beginning to feel better. She was actually looking forward to her meal and was going to do it justice.

Mary had telephoned Miss Broad to let her know that, following the meeting in the classroom, Nicola was going to be all right and also to inform her of the comments made on Facebook.

Over their meal of pork chops, Ben stated that things seemed to have been strange since they had uncovered the trunk. He mentioned that he heard noises at night, as though someone was walking around the house with a walking stick.

"You can hear that too!" exclaimed Abi. Ben nodded.

"I hear it too!" said Nicola.

"Well, I haven't heard anything, have you Mary?" asked Robert. Mary shook her head.

"I think you are all being melodramatic. There is nothing strange going on at all. There will be an explanation for everything," stated Mary. "By the way, I notice you have put that glass vase in the lounge, Abi. Don't you want it in your room?"

Abi swallowed. She had removed the vase from her bedroom windowsill after she had experienced the swirling mist and whispering sounds emanating from it. She had the feeling that somehow the wooden doll and the vase worked off each other if they were kept too close together. When the vase had been out of her room for a while, she had not had any nightmares, but as soon as the vase was back in her room, the whispering and noises had begun again.

"No, I think it looks better in the lounge. Then we can all see it," she replied.

At school the next day, Nicola was drawn to one side by Miss Broad.

"I've had a talk with Lucy's and Stephanie's parents. They are horrified that their girls have been involved in something so cruel. They have asked that they be allowed to deal with it and have also informed me that the Facebook posts have been taken down. I will explain all of this to your mum later, Nicola, but the headmistress is going to give a talk in assembly about being mature when using online sites."

Nicola nodded. She was feeling much better now that she had begun to eat properly again.

"Oh, by the way… Have you heard? Lucy was rushed into hospital last night. It seems she has an acute form of appendicitis. She is really quite poorly," said Miss Broad, before she hurried away to rub the blackboard clean of silly drawings.

Nicola was stunned at this piece of news regarding Lucy. Ben was right. Things were very strange since they had unearthed the trunk. It was as though they had unwittingly unleashed some kind of power. Her eyes strayed to the display board. It was still there. The photo of Lucy and Stephanie. The one with the tack stabbed firmly into the middle of Lucy... and now Lucy was very ill. Nicola thought about her bad dream – she had since recalled it from the other night and wondered... had she signed the book after all?

Chapter Seven

May 1689

The worst has happened. During the night we were attacked. I was woken up with the sounds of my parents' cries of fear. A small band of natives had overrun the homestead. We were all vulnerable in our beds and the natives took full advantage; one in particular, wearing full regalia, consisting of a magnificently feathered headdress and a vividly painted face, set about my parents' bed with his huge axe. I screamed in terror and leaped from my covers, grabbing anything close to hand with which to protect myself. As he advanced, I held up, over my head in a lame attempt to shield it, the Venus Glass. Just as he was about to strike, he stopped short and closely examined the Glass. He seemed mesmerised by it, as though he was watching something, some action, playing out within its depths. Slowly, he let the axe drop to his side, reached across and took the Glass from me. I immediately crouched down and cowered. A trickle of water spread out around my feet as my bladder reacted to my terror.

He studied the Venus Glass for a while, turning it this way and that. I was amazed to see a creamy, luminous, misty light swirling around in its depths. After what seemed like years, he turned his attention back to me, giving me back the Glass and, pulling me up by the arm, marched me outside.

The outbuildings had all been torched and I watched as the homestead suffered the same fate. I was then made to walk behind the native braves, who were on horseback, along with captives collected from some other farms. I recognised no one from our farm.

Slowly, we stumbled along, our eyes smarting from the smoky atmosphere and our lungs scorched from inhaling the fumes of the fires. A few of us were children, and there was a handful of women as well. None of us spoke. We were all too scared to utter a sound.

As dawn broke, we arrived at the natives' camp, having walked through a forest and then out into a clearing close to a river. I could hear the water burbling and tumbling over a rocky bed at a fast rate. The river would be at its fullest, fed by the melting snows of the recent winter.

I was cold, as I only had on my nightdress and my feet were sore and bleeding, their tender skin not equipped to wander the harsh terrain with no protective covering.

The camp itself consisted of tents, or wigwams; conical shapes erected at short notice, and which could be just as quickly taken down again. This small band of Native Americans was transient – a branch of a much larger community, whose more permanent camp was probably much further away.

As we entered the camp, native women and children came to look at us, not with malice in their eyes, but with a genuine interest. The women were immediately concerned with our sorry state, especially those of us who were children. In particular, one fussed over me, taking the Venus Glass from my clutch and wrapping an animal skin around my shoulders to warm me. She led me to her wigwam. I was to find out later that she was the wife of the brave who had killed my parents. Her name was Angeni. Once inside the tent, she asked me to sit down. I was amazed that she could speak English. She quietly attended my sore feet, washing them and then rubbing a gentle herbal paste on them, before wrapping them in binding.

As I began to warm up, I experienced a terrible shaking. It was as though the events of the night were finally making themselves known to me. Over and over I could see, in my head, the forceful swing of the axe, the action of which was the fate of my parents. My teeth rattled and my body shook. The woman gathered me in her arms and gently rocked me back and forth. Gradually I slipped into a black pit of sleep.

Abi looked up from reading the journal and looked at Ricky, Michelle, and then at Nicola and Ben. They were all in the shed. It was the only place they felt they could talk. Abi had suggested her bedroom but Nicola said she didn't want to spend time in there with the wooden doll looking down at them, listening. Normally, Ben would have teased his younger sister for her obvious fear of a doll but he too felt that something weird had escaped when they had opened the trunk.

Michelle, Ben and Nicola still saw the journal as being unreadable and were surprised when Ricky could also read from it – something else unexplainable.

"So," said Ricky. "*Abigail* lost her parents in a native attack. I think I've read that on the internet, somewhere."

"Yes, you have," answered Abi. "Arthur Miller said as much in an interview. I don't know where he got his information from though – there is really nothing recorded about *Abigail*, either before she goes to live at the parsonage with her uncle, or after her last testimony at the witchcraft trials. She just seems to arrive on the scene, create havoc, and then disappear from records."

"I suppose it makes sense that her uncle would want to quickly get her shipped off somewhere as soon as possible. She had done a lot of damage, not least to his reputation," said Ben.

"I think it's time that we ask Mrs Abelman what she knows about all of this. I'm convinced that she has an idea!" exclaimed Abi.

The others nodded. "Why don't we all go and help with the gardening, along with Ben, at the weekend?" suggested Ricky. "Then we could get her talking; ask her a few questions."

They all agreed that this sounded like a plan. Ben said he would check with Mrs Abelman, first, to see whether she minded them descending on her.

Esther alighted from the bus at the depot in Huntingdon and turned to walk in the direction of the care home in which her friend, Muriel, now resided. The evening before, Esther had had a telephone call from Muriel, asking her to visit her the following day, as long as it was convenient. There had been something in the way Muriel spoke which made Esther think that a visit was greatly desired. It sounded as though Muriel needed to get something off her chest, some worry.

It'll be something of nothing, thought Esther. Muriel had overreacted to almost everything that happened in her life. Everything was a drama – especially after... Esther stopped her thoughts from going any further.

Having reached the gates of the home, she turned in and began to walk up the driveway, past the car park, and to the imposing front door. The house had once, in its heyday, been a medium-sized stately manor. It had fallen into disrepair and was purchased by a franchise specialising in the care industry.

It's a very luxuriant setting in which to see out your old age, thought Esther. Although she really couldn't see herself in such a place.

Once inside, she approached the reception desk and asked to see Muriel Harding. She was taken up some stairs and along a corridor. Some of the doors to the bedrooms were open, and as Esther walked past, she couldn't refrain from glancing in. Some residents had visitors; some rooms were empty – their occupants probably sitting in the communal lounge; some housed residents in bed, staring upwards – as though the meaning of life might be posted on the ceiling. She shuddered. It was no fun, getting older and slowly losing your dignity.

Muriel was sitting in an armchair and upon Esther's arrival, she indicated for her to sit in the armchair opposite.

"How are you?" asked Esther, settling herself into the chair and propping the cushion into the small of her back.

"Can't complain," replied Muriel. "I'm glad to see you though, Esther! You're looking quite well. Bring me up to speed with all the gossip back home. How is that new family settling in?"

Esther quickly related all that had been going on in the village, including the spot of intimidation she had recently suffered.

"I know the boy you mean," said Muriel, nodding. "I always thought he looked shifty."

There was a pause in their conversation as the afternoon cuppa was brought around. Esther was also offered a cup. Once the tea had been delivered, they continued their conversation.

Esther sipped her tea. It was lukewarm. A personal hate of hers. Muriel noticed her distaste and laughed.

"It's always cold by the time they get along as far as my room. You need to have a room closer to the kitchens if you want a good hot cuppa!"

"Why don't you complain then?" asked Esther.

Muriel shrugged. "Can't be bothered to," she replied. "Besides, I've got something else to worry about."

Ah-ha, thought Esther. *Here we go.*

"I keep hearing that blessed doll walking about again. Every night. And when I shut my eyes, I keep seeing the vase with its swirling fog. I can't believe I'm hearing and seeing these things in this care home! It's not as though I am living right next door again, is it? I'm a few miles away now, yet I have started to hear and see these strange things. Why now? Has something happened?" asked Muriel, fixing her friend a searching look with her beady eyes.

A starling, thought Esther. *Muriel reminds me of a starling.* Aloud, she said, "They've dug up the trunk."

Muriel sucked in her breath. "What do you mean they? Who's they?" she asked.

"Keep up, Muriel! The family who now live at Jean's, that's who!"

"But why? How?"

Esther rolled her eyes. It was going to be a long afternoon. "Does it matter why or how? They've found it and taken the stuff out of it!" she exclaimed.

Muriel frowned. "I still don't see why they would suddenly take it upon themselves to start digging in that area!" she replied.

"Oh... didn't I say? They've had a pond put in – right in that area, where there are no trees," said Esther.

"Ah," said Muriel. "That explains the discovery. And no, you didn't say. You're getting forgetful, Esther. You'll soon be in here!" she cackled.

"Over my dead body!" said Esther, shuddering.

One of the assistants popped her head round the door. "Everything all right, ladies? You aren't falling out, are you?" she enquired.

Both Esther and Muriel shook their heads, like naughty schoolgirls, and the assistant nodded and disappeared to carry on her many, many errands.

"Have they said anything... You know – like – 'there's some funny comings and goings happening at our house' – to you?" asked Muriel, once they were by themselves again.

"No, they haven't. And I haven't said anything to them either, but I suspect all is not well. I think the children have experienced something – they seem a bit edgy to me – not that I know them that well. It's just a gut feeling I have," replied Esther.

"Well, you need to tell them! Warn them! I thought we had finally put an end to it by burying that doll. And now, I'm right back there, hearing her awful, laboured walking around. It's happened before us, you know, Esther. Someone tried to stop her getting around by chopping her feet off!"

Esther nodded. "Seems there is no way to end this. The doll seems indestructible," she answered.

"You have to find a way, Esther, you have to. I can't stand hearing her at night. It's always at night, when I'm trying to sleep."

"Well, I'll try," said Esther.

Ben was surprised when Mrs Abelman agreed to the others coming over to help with the gardening. He had been worried whether she would find it a bit overwhelming, having them all at her house and had wondered how to broach the subject with her, but he needn't have worried. Mrs Abelman seemed pleased and jumped at the chance to have more visitors and so they agreed that everyone would come round on Saturday.

From Esther's point of view, having promised Muriel that she would try to assist Ben and his family, Esther had pondered how she could best begin a dialogue about the contents of the trunk, so when Ben had asked if she would mind if the others came over to help with the gardening, she thought this too good an opportunity to say no. If truth be told, she was quite looking forward to the company and decided she would bake another cake to celebrate.

At Hinchingbrooke School, Abi was explaining to her teacher her idea for a new version of *The Crucible*. She had finally managed to put down in writing some of her thoughts for the play.

"I must say, Abi, I am very impressed with your idea – it was well worth the wait!" said Miss Jones, grinning. "Just explain to me your thoughts, please."

"Well, I thought it would be interesting to focus on the life of *Abigail Williams* before the witchcraft crisis unfolds – so beginning in 1689. Of course, it would be complete supposition as there is no record of *Abigail* before the witchcraft crisis, or indeed, afterwards. It's as though she is born at around the age of eleven, into the home of *Samuel Parris*, and then disappears sometime during the trials. Also, a crucible is a ceramic or metal melting pot and I wanted to bring forth the theory that the witchcraft crisis was the result of several ingredients being combined to create a recipe of tension and festering resentments which began long before the crisis and culminated in the accusations of witchcraft; those ingredients being; a post-traumatic reaction experienced by some of the Salem Village residents who had been attacked, together with an ongoing fear of attack, by the Native Americans; fear of disease; a discontentment with the parochial leadership – *Reverend Parris* was openly disliked by many of the village residents; and the narrow-minded attitude of many of the Puritans. Also, the crisis grew to envelope residents living in other villages and towns in close proximity to Salem Village," explained Abi.

Miss Jones nodded. "Go on, Abi, I'm liking what I'm hearing!"

"I thought I would begin the play, in the year 1689, with *Abigail* and her parents arriving in New England, from old England, and settling in to help at a farm which *Samuel Parris* – who, by the way, has not yet been appointed reverend to Salem Village – has managed to secure for them and where they would help out with the daily running of the farm. I want to show how *Abigail* may have been one of those people who had suffered some kind of trauma prior to going to live with her uncle in Salem Village. There is some academic thought out there which suggests that *Abigail* witnessed the fatal attack of her parents, though there is nothing concrete to substantiate this. I want the play to be about the lead-up to the events in *The Crucible,* rather than about the trials. I think, what I am trying to say, is that *Abigail* herself was a crucible or a melting pot and was rebelling against the unequal opportunities of her day," said Abi, stopping to gauge the reaction of her teacher.

"I see. So, would the play end with the beginning of the trials, or would you try to document the life of *Abigail* after the trials?" asked Miss Jones.

"No, the play would end just as the trials are to begin – after *Abigail* and the other girls have had their fits," replied Abi. She held her breath and waited to see how Miss Jones reacted to her idea for the play.

"Abi, I think this is a really good idea and I think the Drama department will think so too!" said Miss Jones, clapping her hands together in delight.

On Saturday, the 'gang', as they now liked to think of themselves, met up at Mrs Abelman's. Ricky and Michelle were the first to turn up and they hung about outside, waiting for the others to arrive as they didn't want to have to introduce themselves to Mrs Abelman. It wasn't long before the Williams's arrived. They had taken the shortcut through the woods. On their way, just after they had set off, Nicola had managed to trip up over a boulder, half hidden in the soil.

"Ouch!" she yelled. Her brother and sister, who were walking in front of her, looked back.

"Come on, clumsy," said Ben, grinning and pulling her up.

Nicola brushed the dry leaves off of her clothes and glared at the offending rock. It was a strange shape, with a rounded top and what looked like some figures carved into its face. It was difficult to be sure of the figures as the rock was more than halfway hidden in the soil.

"I've never seen that before," she said, frowning.

"Don't worry about it, it's just some old rock," replied Ben.

Nicola dropped down to one knee and rubbed a little at the rock's face. "It has something carved into it," she said, pointing.

"It's probably an old milestone, or something," said Abi, shrugging her shoulders. "Come on! Whatever it is or was, it's not important. We need to get a move on, the others will be waiting for us."

They carried on their way and eventually came out onto Mrs Abelman's road. As they emerged from the woods, they waved at Ricky and Michelle.

Once all the introductions had been made, the gang made their way into the garden armed with secateurs, hoes, forks and a roll of garden sacks in which to put all the weeds. Esther didn't want the weeds piling onto the compost heap, as that would mean the weeds would be reintroduced to the garden when the compost was ready to be dug back into the soil.

They worked steadily for a couple of hours and then Esther called them in for some tea and a slice of the apple cake she had made only that morning. As the gang entered the kitchen, the smell of baking was still in the air, making all their mouths water in anticipation. The tea, once again served in delicate bone china cups, was hot and reviving for their tired muscles.

"I shall sleep well tonight, after all this exercise and fresh air!" exclaimed Ricky. The others nodded.

After the small talk dried up, there followed a little awkward silence, as no one wanted to be the first to bring up the subject of the trunk. Esther was waiting for them to mention it as she didn't want to appear nosy. Finally, it was Michelle who broke the spell of tension.

"Mrs Abelman, do you know much about the cottage that Abi and her family live in?" she tentatively asked.

Esther nodded. "If you really mean, do I know anything about that trunk which was unfortunately dug up, then yes, I do," she replied.

Everyone remained silent, not wanting to interrupt while Mrs Abelman prepared to begin her story.

"Many years ago, your great grandmother Jean used to attend a charity school in the village of Finedon in Northamptonshire. At this school there was a wooden doll which used to hang on a hook in the entrance hall of the school. It was thought this wooden doll was made around 1912, on the instructions of the then headmistress, Mary

Ozier, to commemorate the two-hundred-year anniversary of the founding of the school in 1712. The doll was carved in the likeness of a girl in Puritan clothing. There was a legend which accompanied the doll. She was said to walk around and in fact many of the girls who were at the school at the same time as Jean, including Jean herself, had, so they say, seen her walking around, usually at night. This legend had been passed along from generation to generation of successive schoolgirls attending Finedon. At some point, prior to Jean's time, someone had obviously tried to stop the doll from getting about because her feet had been chopped off. However, this act didn't succeed because the doll was still heard and seen to be moving around the school at night. She was also used as a form of punishment in that wayward girls would be locked up for a time with the doll in the cellar of the school. Anyway, for some reason, the doll seemed to latch on to Jean in so far as Jean seemed to be plagued the most by the hearing and seeing of her. Jean was tormented for the whole of her time spent at the school. It was a relief for Jean to finally be of an age where she could leave school and begin her adult life. She worked for a time as a maid for a family in Huntingdon, where she also met the man she would marry. The haunting by the doll, as a haunting best describes what went on at the school, according to Jean, had stopped for this period of her life. Then a relative of hers passed away and she was left the cottage in which you now live, and she and her husband moved in. The haunting started again. Which was strange because Jean was nowhere near

Finedon. It was as though the doll could somehow spiritually travel the distance between Warburton and Finedon. Jean never saw her, however, only heard her stomping around at night. As well as hearing the doll, Jean found an old, tatty, diary hidden underneath the floorboards in her bedroom. There was also a vase which, if anything such as flowers were put in it, the flowers died almost immediately. In fact, if anything at all was put into the vase, it was destroyed. It was as though the vase wanted nothing put in it," explained Esther, pausing to look around before she continued with her tale.

"The old book and the vase meant nothing to Jean. These were just items which had been left behind from someone's past life. The haunting by the doll continued until finally Jean could stand it no longer. One night she invited me and my husband and Muriel, the lady who used to live next door to her and her husband, round for dinner. It was during this meal that she first explained to us the legend of the doll. It was a little hard for us to believe at first, but one look at Jean's strained face told us that she was suffering under the weight of it. As the hour approached midnight, and we were still sitting around the table, talking about the doll, we, all of us, heard what had been tormenting Jean. We could hear a slow struggle as though someone was trying to walk with the aid of a walking stick. It was a very disturbing noise and we couldn't tell from which part of the house the sound was coming from. We asked how we could help. It was Jean's husband, Arthur, who came up with a suggestion. You see,

Arthur had lived most of his life in Finedon and so the legend of the doll was well known to him. Granted, he hadn't heard or seen anything of the doll's alleged powers, but he had known enough people who had been terrorised by her to know that this was not just his wife's mind playing tricks on her. Arthur suggested that we steal the doll, which by now was hanging in the church in Finedon, as the school had moved, and the original school building had been sold off and was now a private house. At first, as you can imagine, we were all very reluctant to get involved with theft, but Arthur was very persuasive and so we finally agreed to help." Esther paused again and seemed to be looking inward at her memories. A little while elapsed and Abi was afraid that the old lady was about to forget the rest of the story. One of her clocks struck the hour and this seemed to shake her out of her daydream.

"I remember the date of the theft as though it was yesterday. It was the 18th January 1981 – a Sunday if my memory serves me correctly. Jean's husband, and my husband, Maurice, were the two who went to steal the doll from St Mary's Church in Finedon. Maurice drove our car, which was red, and I remember thinking that it was a very conspicuous colour. Anyway, all went well and they returned safely with the doll. There was uproar in Finedon when the theft was discovered. The police were called in and the theft was reported in the newspaper. It was a very worrying time for us but we sat tight and gradually the furore died down. Unfortunately, poor Muriel let the theft play on her mind and she was never quite the same confident person she had been after that. She became anxious and worried over the silliest of things. Anyway, after the theft, we then put our heads together and wondered how best to destroy the doll. We had tried burning her, but she wouldn't catch fire. We tried sawing her up but, despite her feet having been chopped off in the past, the saw made no mark on her. It was as though she had a protective force around her. In the end, we decided to bury her in an old trunk. Jean also chose this time to get rid of the old book and the vase, both of which gave her the creeps, although, to our knowledge, they had nothing to do with the doll.

"After that, all was quiet. We had succeeded. The haunting had stopped. But now, Muriel tells me that she can hear her again! In the care home! She told me this when I went to visit her. She asked if anything had happened to the trunk so I had to tell her you had dug it up. She's really worried for you," explained Esther, taking a sip of tea from her cup. Unfortunately it had gone cold.

A reflective silence followed Esther's story.

"I can understand not being able to work out where in the house the noise comes from. I have the same problem," said Abi, looking at Ben and Nicola for back-up. They each nodded. "But I have no idea how the doll fits into our story. She definitely has something to do with the vase, because I feel they feed off of each other in some way. Ricky and I can read from the diary, you know. To us, the book is in a legible condition and seems to be the memoirs of *Abigail Williams* – you know – the girl in *The Crucible?"* said Abi to Esther.

Esther nodded. "Yes, I know the play by Arthur Miller. But she was in America, wasn't she? What has she to do with Jean's cottage?

"Apparently, after the Salem witch tragedy, she was sent back to England in disgrace," said Ricky, joining in the conversation. "We haven't read the whole of the journal yet. Maybe there are some answers in it."

"What has *Abigail* to do with the wooden doll?" said Abi, frowning. "You're right, Ricky. I think we need to hurry up and read the rest of the journal."

Chapter Eight

July 1689

I have been living with the natives for a good many weeks and I have been well looked after. Angeni, who had taken me in and bandaged my feet, was a settler who had been captured as a child. Angeni was her native name and she told me it meant spiritual angel. Apparently my name, when shortened to Abey, meant leaf. She also had been well looked after and as no one had come to rescue her, she grew up amongst the natives and adopted their way of life. Her son, Takamunna, was a couple of years older than me and I grew to adore him. He could speak my language as his mother had taught him. He would take me with him into the forest and show me which berries I could eat. He also took me to a shallow part of the river and taught me how catch fish by tickling them out of the water.

One day, Takamumma and I were coming back from just such a journey, our catch of the day strung onto a stick and swinging as Takamumma carried it across his shoulder. As we came into the camp, one of the old ladies who had been captured nearly a year ago, came up to me and slapped me across the face. She was disgusted with the way I carried on with the 'godless heathens'. She pulled my hair, which was loose and uncovered, and told me to cover it up and act like a Puritan girl. I was surprised by the depth of my feelings towards her. I hated her. I think Takamunna could see into my heart and knew how I felt because he pulled me along with him, back to the family wigwam.

Takamunna's father, Wamsutta, the native who had been responsible for the death of my parents, kept his distance from me, I think out of a kind of respect for my feelings. However, one afternoon, I was sitting on the bank of the river, by myself, when he approached me. He had something hidden behind his back and, at first, I was alarmed. I needn't have been, because he produced a wonderful wooden carving of a Puritan girl and she carried a Bible and a scroll. He said he had carved her in my likeness and that he had put a spell on her, charging her with the order to look after me as I no longer had parents. I accepted the gift.

That night, as I prepared to go to bed, it felt as though my mother was brushing my hair, the way she used to when she was alive, and as I lay down to sleep, a voice, deep inside my head, wished me a goodnight. Was it the doll?

Abi couldn't believe what she was reading. The wooden doll *Abigail* mentioned in her journal was surely the same wooden doll which had been stolen from the Finedon church? It was too much of a coincidence not to be. In which case, the doll was much older than anyone realised. Perhaps the headmistress of the charity school in 1912 had merely found the doll, instead of having her made?

Abi lay in her bed and considered these possibilities. It was late and she knew she should be getting some sleep, but the lure of the journal was keeping her wide eyed and alert. She plumped up her pillow, snuggled down between the covers and carried on reading.

The days in the camp carried on in much the same way. I found that I loved living this kind of life. Granted, it was through the summer months and the weather was warm – I think it would have seemed more of a hardship during the harsh winter. I liked the loving atmosphere under which the native children were nurtured. There were rules which they had to obey, but if a child was naughty, their parents would sit them down and tell a story which outlined the reason why the child's behaviour was unacceptable. Feelings were also allowed to be expressed and everything was altogether much more relaxed than the upbringing I had had.

I was also surprised to learn that they observed religion too. Some of the natives had become Christian but they still remembered their own religion. Also, the way the religions were taught was much more interesting and vibrant, compared with the way we Puritans had to learn. There was no having to read the Scriptures every night and my Puritan world seemed to lack colour.

After Wamsutta had given me the doll, things between us were a little easier. Takamunna had helped me to understand the way of the land. He told me that some settlers had killed Wamsutta's parents when he was a boy and that it was the settlers who had brought a more aggressive style of attack with them and the natives were merely fighting like with like. It helped me to balance my feelings between the horror of losing my parents and my happiness at living in the camp. I did not care if no one came to rescue me. In this respect, I was like Takamunna's mother, Angeni.

However, my Uncle Parris, who had finally taken up position as reverend to Salem Village in June, visited the camp. He had collected together a posse of menfolk and, having found out where I had been taken, brought along some native hostages which had been captured by the settlers, and swapped me and others for the native hostages and we were allowed to go home. I was very upset at leaving Takamunna, but I had no choice. Uncle would not hear of me staying behind to continue to live with the natives. The old lady who had slapped me across the face was also being freed and I saw her talking to my uncle, no doubt informing him of my unseemly behaviour and how I had disgraced them all by making myself at home among the natives.

As I left the camp with my few belongings, including the wooden doll and my glass vase, Takamunna rushed up to me and gave me a beaded amulet in the shape of a lizard. He explained to me that he had been given the charm on the day he had been born and it was supposed to protect him through his life. He said he wanted me to have it, so it would protect me until the day when he would find me again and be able to look after me himself. I was very touched by this act of kindness and it made our separation from each other a little easier.

I wasn't looking forward to life with Uncle Parris and his family. For a start, I had never met my aunt and their children. How would I fit in? Would I be able to be a good Puritan girl, now that I had had the natives' culture to compare it with? These thoughts plagued me and I looked to the next episode in my life with trepidation.

Abi reluctantly closed the journal. It made for very good reading, but she realised she needed to sleep or she would be nodding off at school. Before she turned off her light, she cast a glance at Peg, the wooden doll, hanging from her hook on the wall. The nights had been free of her walking and clumping around and Abi wondered why. What was it that made the doll embark on her nightly travels?

Josh Harrison was dreaming. He was asleep in his bed in his room at the Halls of Residence at University. The subject of his dream was Michelle's friend, Abi – which, somewhere in his subconscious, surprised him, as he hadn't given her a thought! In his dream he was in her bedroom, sitting on the end of her bed and she was lying in bed, her long, golden, luxurious hair spread invitingly across her pillow…

Josh sat up in his own bed, his heart hammering in his chest. *No,* his mind screamed, *she is way too young, under age even.* He ran his fingers through his hair, clicked on his lamp and reached for his bottle of water which he kept at the side of his bed. As he unscrewed the cap and took a gulp, he realised he was trembling… with fear…? or something else…? He wasn't sure. He closed his eyes and tried to bring forth the face of Susie, but the memory of Abi's face kept getting in the way. *This is all wrong,* he told himself sternly. *Get a grip and settle down.*

After a bit of deep breathing exercise, Josh felt calm enough to turn the light off and try to resume sleep. *There's no harm done,* he thought. *It was, after all, only a dream. I love Susie and I would never act in such a despicable way.* He closed his eyes, but the nagging question remained – *where did the dream come from?*

The light from the lamp he had switched on was of a very dim quality, more of a nightlight, in truth. Its circle of illumination only stretched as far as to the middle of his bed. If the light had been more powerful, he might have noticed the translucent figure, about a meter in height, standing in the corner of his room. As it happened, he was blissfully unaware of the wooden doll who watched him, her carved lips forming a little knowing smile. *My Abigail wants you, Josh. It's just a matter of time,* she gently whispered.

Mary unlocked the front door of her house, shook out her umbrella before closing it down, and hurried into the hallway, closing the door behind her. What a day to have to pop out to the shop. They had run short of bread and so she had made a quick trip round to the village shop to buy some more. She didn't mind too much as it was nice to be able to support the local business. On entering the shop, she had come upon two men having quite a heated argument over their differing views of Brexit. The two men in question had been lifelong friends, but had voted in opposition and now they were sworn enemies – a mounting problem which seemed to be reflected nationally. Mary thought it was quite sad that such a huge question had been asked of the nation and it had only served to split opinion, more or less, right down the middle. The overall atmosphere of the village had been affected too and something, some quaint innocence, had disappeared.

She switched the radio on for a bit of company and set about her chores. The ten o'clock news came on and she was interested to note that some virus had been discovered in Wuhan City in China. *How dreadful,* she thought. *At least we don't have that problem here.*

As she went past the lounge, she noticed a peculiar smell coming from it and so went in to investigate. The fresh flowers she had put in the tear-shaped vase, only yesterday, were dead and the water was a horrible dark green with a stagnant smell. She removed the vase to the kitchen and wrapped the offending flowers in newspaper. She took them and the vase outside, braving the rain, and put the flowers in the bin and poured the water straight down the drain. Once back inside, she then washed the vase, taking care to rub away the horrible green water line on the inside of the vase. She dried it and returned the vase to the lounge, speculating as to why the flowers had died so quickly and why the water had turned stagnant. *Perhaps it was too hot for them in here?* she questioned herself. But then she remembered how the potpourri she had put in the vase had gone slimy. She frowned at the vase, but then shrugged. *It's just one of those things,* she thought to herself.

Left by itself, the atmosphere inside the vase began to thicken and swirl. A mist developed and, just briefly, formed a face which housed yellow wolf-like eyes, which were soon swallowed up in the fog.

Nicola brought her two friends home with her after school. It was the last day of the autumn term and the schools were breaking up for the Christmas holidays. Both Lucy, who was now fully recovered from her appendicitis operation, and Stephanie, had apologised to her and had asked for her forgiveness. Not wanting to remain without friendship, however two-faced it might be, Nicola had accepted their apologies and things seemed to be back to normal.

Mary, on the other hand, was not so forgiving and she was finding it very hard to be nice and welcoming towards the two girls. She felt she was speaking to them through gritted teeth. It was with relief that she was able to turn her attention to Abi and Ben, who had arrived home together.

"What are they doing here?" asked Ben. "Please tell me that Nick hasn't forgiven them!" Ben, who had returned to school a few weeks ago, had let Jamie know that he no longer wanted to be a part of his gang and he was slowly making new friends and felt all the happier for it.

Mary shrugged her shoulders. "They are staying for tea," she explained.

"What!" he exclaimed. "So we have to make polite conversation round the table, do we? Don't know if I can."

"You have to, for Nicola's sake," explained Abi. "I know, it won't be easy."

Mary went into the lounge to switch on the fairy lights on the Christmas tree. Abi and Ben went upstairs to their rooms.

Abi opened the door to her bedroom, just as Lucy was coming out of the bathroom, which was next door. She glanced in at Abi's room and noticed the wooden doll hanging on the wall.

"So, you still like dolls too! Must run in the family," she giggled, but the message in her eyes was pure spite. Abi felt her temper rising, but managed to swallow it. She wished Nicola had the courage to sever her relationship with Lucy. It was rumoured that Lucy might be going to a private school next September and Abi fervently hoped that this would be the case.

There was another curious atmosphere around the dinner table that night. Robert and Ben refused to engage with the two girls and so it was left to Abi and Mary to make small talk and the meal seemed to drag on.

Abi thankfully closed her bedroom door. She had got ready for bed almost straight after dinner was finished. She wanted to try to read a lot more of *Abigail's* journal and also she couldn't bear to be in the company of Nicola's friends a moment longer. As she was propping up her pillow against the headboard, a text arrived on her phone. Idly she opened it. It was from Michelle, informing her that Josh was staying at the vicarage for Christmas and that she thought it only fair, given how Abi had felt about him, that she let her know, to avoid any potential embarrassment. Abi texted back her thanks and said she was grateful that Michelle was trying to protect her feelings.

Hmm... Josh, thought Abi and for some reason she looked up at the wooden doll. Peg seemed to hold Abi's gaze and a slight smile hovered around her wooden lips. Abi blinked and looked again – the doll's expression was back to normal. *I'm losing it,* thought Abi. *I don't know what to think anymore. It all seems too fantastic.*

She picked up the journal and turned to the page where she had last left off reading. *Abigail* had arrived at the vicarage and had settled into the Parris family life. Her aunt and cousins had welcomed her with enough warmth to settle any misgivings which *Abigail* had harboured. Her cousin *Betty* was two years younger than *Abigail,* but, in spite of this, the two girls became firm friends.

January 1692

All is not well. I sense friction within the village. Uncle Samuel is not liked by a good many of the village people. I am not surprised. He manages, with his sermons, to ostracise certain people of the congregation who are not full members of the church. They come to the meetinghouse and listen to the sermons but are asked.... no... they are ordered, to leave on sacrament days so that the members can take communion together. He has also denied the baptism of infants born to non-members, even though the parents in question have themselves been baptised when they were children. The result is that the non-members are now refusing to contribute towards their share of Uncle's salary or to supply him with firewood. This, in turn, has made my uncle's sermons even more full of acid than before. He uses his sermons to plant the seed that the devil walks among the non-members. All of this makes for a very unsettled, unloving and non-inclusive atmosphere, just at a time when we should all be pulling together. I have to admit, it makes me sick to my stomach. Having witnessed, first hand, the warm and inclusive attitude of the supposedly, godless heathens, which are the natives, I cannot help but think we have much to learn from them.

Life at the parsonage would seem very grey but for the existence of one person. Tituba. She is of Native American appearance but I think she comes from further afield – brought to the New World from Barbados by my uncle. She is colourful and she makes me laugh. Betty and I bully her into telling us about her childhood. She gathers us around, when my aunt and uncle are not at home, and tells us stories which send shivers down our spines. Hers was a childhood full of magic and voodoo and she tells us about it in whispers, just in case my uncle arrives home suddenly. He would certainly punish her with the whip if he were to hear such profanity uttered in the walls of the parsonage. On some occasions, we are joined by Anne Putnam, a friend of mine who is around the same age as me.

Tituba makes a special concoction. I think this is to help with childbearing. I often see the designated village midwife secretly taking possession of a bottle of something which Tituba has made. I once challenged Tituba on this and she admitted to making a brew, from a recipe handed down from wise woman to wise woman, made from the fungal growth on rye and sweetened with honey and mint. Its name begins with a 'K' ... but I have forgotten what she called it. I remember my mother telling me that it was rumoured Jane Throckmorten had drunk some concoction she found hidden under the bed of the maid who worked for her family. Apparently, Jane had taken a little of this medicine to help bring on her fits and hallucinations. I once asked my mother how such a story had survived nearly one hundred years! She had answered me by tapping her nose and then told me to hurry up with my chores. I never did fully understand how or why this story has echoed down through the decades.

One day, Betty and I were bored. We had completed all of our chores and we had the parsonage to ourselves. Betty asked me if we could do an oomancy, using my glass vase. She wanted to find out if she was to marry Benjamin, the boy she had her eye on. Knowing that this would make Uncle Samuel very angry, should he ever find out, I gladly agreed. The idea of doing an oomancy behind his back in his parsonage filled me with delight.

However, things did not quite happen as planned. Tituba, who had been on an errand, came home earlier than expected and she was not happy to find us carrying on in such a way. Her eyes bulged when she saw the egg white in the glass and both she and Betty reacted badly when they both thought they could see that the shape of a coffin had formed in the water. I did not share their opinion of the coffin shape. To me it just looked like a mass of egg white. Then Tituba was convinced that the head of my wooden doll had turned to look at her! Which made me wonder whether Tituba had been secretly drinking her own hidden brew! Betty became very agitated and was worried that her father might return any minute – a worry shared by Tituba, who was also convinced that Uncle Samuel, or the Master, as she called him, would blame her for the oomancy and punish her for it. So we quickly tidied up, pouring the egg white and water outside onto the soil, making sure that no suspect white was left on top of the soil by burying it. The doll was stored away under our bed. Uncle Samuel did not like my doll, despite the fact that she was Puritan and carried the Bible and a scroll. He never asked where she came from or who had carved her. He probably had his suspicions that a native had made her. Overall, it was best to keep her hidden away out of his sight.

It was after this that Betty turned very peculiar. She would not let it rest that she had been deceitful and she worried that Tituba, in an effort to protect her own interests, might well tell Uncle about coming home and finding us in the middle of performing an oomancy. I had to admit that maybe Betty had a point. Tituba was acting strangely herself. She seemed very nervous and would jump out of her skin if anyone was a little quiet in their approach to her and she hadn't seen them. She would do anything to avoid being punished and it may have been that she was worried we would tell my uncle that the oomancy was her idea. Therefore, a vast wall of mistrust grew up between us.

I had an idea, which came from the stories my mother used to tell me about Jane Throckmorten. We needed my uncle to believe we had been bewitched. That way we could ensure pity and sympathy, rather than harsh words and punishment. It would be harmless as we wouldn't name anyone specific and so no one would be hurt by our plan. Betty agreed, after much pushing on my part. We decided to look under Tituba's bed, which was in the corner of the room she shared with myself and Betty, and try to find the secret brew which I knew she had freshly made just the other day. As far as I could tell, no one had come to claim the mixture as yet. We waited until Tituba had been sent out to gather fallen bits of wood and pine cones, to help eke out our meagre store of firewood. This was a task both Betty and myself had been told to do on many occasions and it was both time consuming and tedious and the end result only gave rise to a small amount of heat.

As soon as Tituba left for her wood-scavenging duty, Betty and I hurried upstairs and fished underneath the little, low wooden bed on which Tituba slept and snored every night. There was a basket, covered over with a cloth, which we dragged out. Gently, we pulled away the cloth and peered into the depths of the basket. The stoppered bottle of substance was in there and we took it out, making sure to put the basket back as and where we had found it. We then sat down on our bed and studied the bottle.

"I don't want to drink it," said a worried Betty. "What if it does me some harm?"

"It won't do you any long-term harm, Betty. My mother said Jane Throckmorten took it and she was fine. It just makes you see the devil's helpers and their familiars and makes your body twist into funny shapes, that's all."

"That's all!" Betty had said aggressively. "If that's all, then you take some first, Abigail Williams, and see how you like it!"

I had hurriedly put my fingers to my lips as a sign that Betty should be quieter. "Very well. Let's both take it then," I had suggested. "But once we start, we must keep up the pretence or we will be in even more trouble than we are now," I had further said, in a warning tone.

Abi stopped reading at this point. So, the witchcraft incident started off as a prank to hide the fact that the girls had been dabbling in a less than pure pastime. That they were, or at least *Betty* was, terrified of being exposed as a deceitful daughter, was obvious. *But what,* thought Abi, *did this say about Samuel Parris? He had made himself some enemies in the Village, but he also had a lot of supporters. He seemed, from Abigail's description, to be a man who did not take lightly to being crossed and both his daughter and Tituba were clearly very afraid of him. If he lived today, would he be seen as abusive?*

Abi wanted to carry on reading, but she was aware of her eyes beginning to close and of reading the same sentence over and over, so she reluctantly closed the journal and put it to one side. It wasn't long before she was asleep.

Josh Harrison was also asleep, in his bed in the vicarage. He was laying on his back, looking the very picture of contentment. Suddenly his eyes flew open and he sat up in bed, shoving the duvet to one side as he did so. He got out of bed, his eyes fixed somewhere in the distance and the expression in them was glazed. Josh was still asleep. He slipped his feet into his boots, not bothering to tie them up, and walked to the bedroom door and opened it, walked through it and left it open behind him. As he descended the stairs, he was not bothered to try and move stealthily out of deference to others asleep in the vicarage. The stairs creaked and groaned their annoyance at being disturbed so late at night. Reaching the front door, he stretched up and drew back the bolt at the top and then bent to jiggle the bolt at the bottom of the door. Turning the key, he opened the door and stepped out into the cold night. He left the front door open, to swing to and fro in the slight night breeze. Wearing only his pyjama bottoms, he set off down the road and cut into the woods. He walked like a zombie, his expression never changing, even when a thorny branch smacked him across the face. On he walked. A man on a mission.

Finally he arrived at his destination. Abi's garden. He stood gazing up at her bedroom window. The curtains were drawn. The entire house was in darkness. Bending down, he scooped up a handful of little pebbles and began to throw them, one by one, at her bedroom window. Suddenly, the curtains were disturbed and a tousled head could be seen looking down at the person in the garden.

Abi, unable to believe the sight she was seeing, opened her bedroom window and quietly called down.

"Josh!" she whispered loudly. "What on earth…?"

Josh said nothing, just stood in the garden, like a robot awaiting further command and Abi became aware that something was wrong. Closing her window, she quickly donned her dressing gown and hurriedly pulled on her soft and furry, booty-style slippers, tucking the legs of her pyjamas into them.

Hurrying down the stairs, she was careful to avoid the bottom step as it always creaked and, at this time of night, would sound like a gun going off. She did not want to arouse the rest of the family. She grabbed her dad's anorak from the coat rack.

Once outside, she cautiously approached Josh. She had read somewhere that it could be harmful to suddenly wake up a sleepwalker. She was sure that this was Josh's current state and one look at his eyes confirmed her suspicions. She gently wrapped the anorak around his shoulders and as she did so, he reached for her, running his fingers through her hair and tilting her head back so he could kiss her. It all happened so suddenly. His mouth was warm and she found herself responding before coming to her senses and pulling back. His arms dropped to his sides, but the same glazed look still haunted his eyes. He was still asleep.

I'd better get him home, thought Abi. She turned him around and began to lead him back through the woods. When they arrived at the vicarage, she was relieved to see that the front door was open. There appeared to be no one up and wondering where Josh was, so he must have left the door open. Together, they entered the vicarage. Abi was worrying as to which would be Josh's room and, even more alarming, would he be sharing it with Susie? Getting him back into bed without disturbing her would be impossible and what story should Abi tell her?

As they made their way upstairs, Abi noticed one of the bedroom doors was open, so she presumed this was his room. She quietly peered around the door to check whether Susie was sleeping in there. The bed was empty. It appeared that Josh slept alone.

Of course, thought Abi. *I remember Michelle saying that her dad was like a relic from the Victorian era and that he didn't like unmarried couples sharing a room under his roof. Phew! That certainly makes my task tonight a lot easier.*

Abi managed to take Josh's boots off and to get him to lay down in his bed and she tucked him up, hoping that he would soon warm up. As she was struggling to put her dad's anorak on over her dressing gown, for added warmth, during her journey back home, the bedroom door was pushed open wider.

"Whatever is going on in here?" asked a voice.

Chapter Nine

Abi slowly turned around to face whoever had come into the room. She was relieved to see that it was Michelle.

"Oh, Shell, thank goodness it's only you!" she quietly exclaimed, putting her finger to her lips and moving to close the bedroom door.

"As opposed to who? Susie?" asked Michelle, folding her arms angrily.

Abi stopped trying to get the second of her enormous furry cladded arms into the sleeve of her dad's anorak, and her jaw dropped in surprise at the suspicious tone present in Michelle's voice.

Michelle cast a critical eye over her friend, her expression taking in Abi's slippers, pyjamas and dressing gown and the half-worn anorak. "I see you couldn't be bothered to dress for the occasion," she said with a clipped voice.

"What? No! You have it all wrong. This isn't what it looks like. Trust me, Michelle, please. He was sleepwalking. I was looking out for him. Look, now's not the time to discuss this. We will wake up the whole household in a minute, if we're not careful," replied Abi.

Michelle looked unconvinced and regarded Abi through narrow eyes.

"I'm just going to go on home and I will tell you everything tomorrow. Please don't say anything to anyone, including Josh. I promise I'll tell you tomorrow," pleaded Abi.

Michelle sighed. There had to be a rational explanation as to why her best friend was in her sister's boyfriend's bedroom at two in the morning. Josh wasn't even awake and Abi would never be so underhanded. "Okay. I'll give you the benefit of the doubt, for the moment... but your explanation had better be good!"

Abi heaved a sigh of relief. "I'm going now. Let's agree to meet at the shed tomorrow morning at about eleven o'clock, shall we?"

Michelle nodded. "Wait!" she whispered, as Abi was creeping out of the bedroom. "Isn't it a bit risky, you know, going home at this time on your own? Have you got your phone with you?"

Abi shook her head. "I didn't think to pick it up. Don't worry. I'll be fine. Home isn't far away."

"Text me as soon as you get home. I'll give you twenty minutes and if I don't receive your text, then I'm sounding the alarm," replied Michelle.

Both girls had, by now, quietly descended the stairs and Michelle closed and bolted the front door after her friend had left. She stood for a while with her back resting against the door, listening. No one in the house, it seemed, had been disturbed by the nighttime visitor, including

Josh. This worried Michelle and so she checked in on him on her way back to bed. He seemed peaceful enough and his body temperature felt normal to the touch and he flinched a little in his sleep, when she put her hand on his forehead. Reassured, Michelle went back to bed and waited for Abi to send her text.

As Abi made her way home, through the woods, she reflected on how quiet the weather was. There was no breeze and everything was very still. It seemed as if the night was waiting for something to happen, as though it was holding its breath. Strangely, she found this more unsettling than if there had been a howling storm, complete with thunder and lightning, as happens in all the good horror stories. She drew her dad's anorak up around her neck and hurried on her way. It had been a bad choice to wear her slippers, even though they had a decent rubber sole on them. The creamy artificial fur was now filthy. She would have been better borrowing her dad's wellies. She hadn't had time to really think things through. At least Josh was back in his bed and out of harm's way. Abi wondered if his sleep-walking was a regular occurrence. On and on these thoughts cannoned around in her head, keeping her company through the lonely walk home. Suddenly, she came to a dead standstill. Someone close by was crying. Fear turned Abi's stomach over. What should she do? Did someone need help, or was it better to run on home?

She peered through the woods. There was enough moonlight to be able to see. As far as she could tell, the crying was coming from the place where Nicola had fallen over the stone. Abi could just make out the shape of the boulder. There was someone sitting on the ground by it, their back to her. Whoever it was, they were wearing a cloak and had the hood pulled up over their head. Abi approached carefully.

"Hello. Everything alright?" she asked, through chattering teeth.

The crying stopped and slowly the person turned to look at her. Abi got a shock! It was like looking in a mirror. Except for the grey wavy hair which was protruding from the hood, the face of the woman looking back at her was an older version of her own!

The woman got up and began to walk towards Abi. "He should not be here!" she said vehemently, all the while getting closer to Abi. "He should not be here! *He should not be here!*" she screamed in Abi's face. Abi closed her eyes and waited for whatever assault was coming her way. Nothing happened and slowly she dared to open her eyes. No one was there. The woman had vanished without a trace. Abi didn't hang around and ran the rest of the way to her house. Happy to find the front door was still unlocked as she had left it, she quickly went in, closed and locked it. She sat on the bottom step of the stairs to get her breath back and calm her shaking body... but then remembered she had to text Michelle or all hell would break lose. She hurried up the stairs to her bedroom, grabbed her phone and quickly rattled off a message to her friend, telling her she was home safe and sound. Michelle responded with a thumb's up emoji.

It was bedlam in the Williams's household the following morning. It was just a couple of days before Christmas and everyone wanted to wrap their presents at the same time. There was only one roll of sticking tape and so this made a perfect scenario for the three siblings to fall out.

"Oh, for goodness' sake!" exclaimed Abi, as Nicola came into her bedroom and snatched the tape away just as Abi was about to reach for it. She let go of the paper she was trying to hold in place around a package and it immediately unfolded itself, flicking off bits of its silver twinkle as it did so. She decided to give it up as a bad job. She would visit the village store later, after her meeting with Michelle, and buy herself some tape.

At five to eleven, she popped down to the shed and opened up. No one had been in there for a few weeks and the spiders had taken over. Abi brushed away a cobweb hanging across the doorway and went in. Sitting down on one of the chairs, she glanced at her watch and then waited for Michelle to turn up. It was about ten past eleven when her friend finally arrived.

"Sorry I'm a bit late," Michelle apologised. "I tried to do too many jobs and ran out of time."

"S'okay," replied Abi. "You're here now."

"So, go on then… whatever was going on last night?" asked Michelle.

Abi had mentally rehearsed what she was going to say to Michelle. She had decided on the truth. The situation was already bizarre enough without complicating it further by telling a series of lies. Why lie anyway? It wasn't as though she needed to cover her tracks – she hadn't done anything wrong! So she set to and explained everything which had happened in the small hours of the morning. She explained about the kiss and how strange and other worldly Josh had seemed. Stranger still, was the kiss itself... delivered by someone who was still asleep and who would have no memory of it! Abi was thankful for that in one respect... yet disappointed on another level. However, she decided to leave out the strange incident which happened in the woods on the way home. This was not really part of the 'Josh' story, strictly speaking, and it would save for another time, when the rest of their gang were together.

When she had finished explaining the events to Michelle, there was silence while her friend digested all that she had heard. "Well," she finally said. "I don't know what to make of that. I don't think Susie knows that Josh is prone to sleepwalking. I wonder if Josh even knows? How do we tell him?"

Abi shrugged. "I know I've called it sleepwalking, but somehow, it seemed more like he was under some sort of influence."

"What... you mean like drugs?" asked a shocked Michelle.

"No! More like he was a puppet and someone was in charge of his strings, or a robot, or something like that, waiting for some further command," explained Abi. "How did he seem this morning, anyway?"

Michelle shrugged. "I don't know, I haven't seen him. Everyone else is fine though. No one, Susie for one, seems at all worried about him, so I'm guessing he has no memory of last night and is carrying on as though nothing happened."

"Well, at least that's something. What do we do? Do we tell him or shall be wait to see if it happens again, and then tell him?" asked Abi.

Michelle quickly looked at her watch. "Look, let's leave well enough alone for now and see what transpires. At least we are aware of a slight problem. I haven't got the time to give it proper consideration right now – I have to go, as I promised my dad I would help clean and tidy the church ready for Christmas."

Abi nodded and made ready to leave the shed as well. Together the girls locked up and Abi said she would walk with Michelle so far, and then walk on to the shop to buy her tape.

On her way back home, a small roll of sticking tape having been purchased, Abi decided to pop in and see Esther.

"Oh, this is a nice surprise!" said Esther on opening her front door. "Come on in. I've just made some chocolate chip cookies and I'll put the kettle on for a brew."

Abi followed her into the warm and cosy kitchen and sat in the cushioned window seat, removing her jacket and scarf. Esther busied herself, putting on the kettle and setting out her delicate bone china cups on a tray. She added the milk jug and sugar bowl and placed her newly baked chocolate chip cookies on a plate.

"So, how are things at home?" she asked Abi. "How is the wooden doll?"

"She's been rather quiet these past few nights. None of us has heard her stomping around. I don't know whether to relax or be alarmed!" replied Abi, laughing. She gratefully accepted her cup of tea and helped herself to a cookie. She paused and quietly studied Esther. She wanted to ask her about her time in Germany when she was a young girl. Ben had mentioned it to Abi in passing but now Abi was a little concerned that the topic might be too personal. The last thing she wanted to do was to cause offence. Perhaps she could try the gentle approach.

"Mrs Abelman?" she began, tentatively. "Ben told me that you seemed confused and that you thought you were back in Germany, when he and mum found you in our next-door neighbour's garden and I just wondered why you thought that?"

Esther regarded Abi for a moment before answering her. "You can call me Esther, by the way. Calling me 'Mrs Abelman' makes me feel old. Yes, I remember I was acting a little strange when your mum and brother found me. The whole episode took me right back to when I was a little girl, when we lived in Germany."

"What happened to you? Don't talk about it, if it's too personal. I'm just interested," asked Abi.

"No, it's not too personal. My family had lived in Germany for many, many decades. One of my uncles had fought in the Great War, on the side of Germany, and had earned himself a medal of honour. We considered ourselves to be German in every way, but we were also Jewish. This wasn't a problem until after the Wall Street Crash of 1929, which caused a deep economic downturn on an international scale and led to the Great Depression.

"After the Great War was finished, the countries of France, Great Britain, and Germany were on their knees, financially. There was much anger and Germany was made to sign the Treaty of Versailles and to accept the entire blame, rightly or wrongly, for the war and to pay for all the damage – in other words, to make reparations. The cost of reparations was set to an enormous level and would take Germany until the 1980s to pay in full. On top of this, she was only allowed to have a small military, enough, really, with which to defend herself, and there were other restrictions applied, too. The United States lent money to help Europe rebuild itself and things for Germany, during the 1920s, were looking up. However, after the Wall Street Crash, the USA recalled all debts and this, for Germany, caused massive unemployment and hyperinflation. The country was brought to the brink of disaster and, as tends to happen during hard times, a scapegoat is needed – someone to blame for all that is wrong. It was the Jewish community which bore the brunt of the festering anger which was being fanned by Adolph Hitler and the Nazi party. As Germany's surrender at the end of the Great War was handled by, among others, a Jewish person, Hitler used this as a means to denigrate our whole people. He put the blame of Germany's surrender and therefore the signing of the hated Treaty, squarely at the feet of the Jewish community and because people, generally, have to have someone to blame, his message hit home.

"People turned against us. People we had known all our lives no longer wanted to have anything to do with us and worse, they actively began to persecute us. We no longer felt safe just walking down the road and, as the Nazi message penetrated minds, we had bricks thrown through our windows. As you can imagine, as a young girl, I found this bewildering. I was terrified. It is horribly unsettling to feel unsafe in your own home.

"If my father had not made his decision to remove us to somewhere safer, I would not be talking to you today. We would have perished in the concentration camps. As it was, we did lose cousins and aunts and uncles."

Abi reflected on this for a moment. "Society seems to have to blame someone and it's happened right down through the ages. Something, some catastrophe occurs, and the majority looks for who is the cause of it."

Esther nodded in agreement. "Where else has it happened, then, in your opinion, Abi?" she asked.

"Well, I was thinking specifically of the Salem Witch Trials. The settlers were having a hard life, and bad things just kept happening to them and instead of looking to themselves and understanding that maybe the way they treated each other, along with their fear of the natives, was the real cause, they believed God was angry with them and was teaching them a lesson by allowing the Devil to entice and corrupt certain members of their society. The question for them was who? Who had been corrupted, and so they engulfed themselves in narrow-minded attitudes and spied on each other and told tales on each other – tales of fantasy which others were only too pleased to believe because it suited them. The people in authority in that day fanned the flames of superstition because it focused the public's eye on these, so say, corruptions and away from the fact that the authorities were failing to provide its people with a safe haven. In other words, the local authorities were only too glad to be able to hide their failings behind such superstitions."

Esther nodded her agreement again. "It happens time and again. We, as a race, were not being accused of witchcraft, of course – that sort of thinking had died out a long time ago – but persecution is persecution however you want to dress it up. It happens whenever times are hard – when unemployment is high and food is scarce. Frustrations are taken out on the most vulnerable in society. Of course, as Jewish people, we hadn't had a homeland for such a long time and there were pockets of us to be found scattered across all countries – 'the Diaspora of Jews exiled from Israel by the Babylonians,' as the Bible refers to it. So we have never truly been accepted by any of these countries, however long a Jewish person can claim his family has lived in a particular country. It wasn't just in Germany we have been persecuted either. There have been pogroms in Russia too and in other countries. We are the world's whipping boy – when the economy is flourishing, we are tolerated but when times are not so good, we bear the brunt of ill will."

"I suppose the Jewish experience is a little different to the Witch Trials in that I think that certain people in Salem Village were able to make gains out of others' miseries – in some of the cases, I think it was greed which made people discredit their neighbours. They were able to grab land or some other booty for themselves," replied Abi.

"What! Do you think no one benefitted from the enforced denial of our civil rights and liberties? What about all the businesses and artwork and homes and money which were stripped from us and appropriated by the Nazis? It all disappeared, you know – stashed away into their private bank accounts."

"I hadn't thought about it like that, Esther. It seems people manipulate others into terrible acts whilst they themselves sit back and line their own pockets!" replied Abi.

"Oh yes! God does allow the Devil to play amongst us. The shame of it is that we are unable to see who the real demons are. The real evil in Salem Village did not live in those poor people who were hanged as witches – they were innocent – the true demons were those who accused them of witchcraft!" exclaimed Esther.

Abi thought about this. Was *Abigail* evil? Or was she merely trying to expose the hypocrisy of her society and it all got out of hand? Had she meant for innocent people to be hung or did she see all of her society as being at fault, with their narrow-minded thoughts and attitudes. Was she working for the Devil or was she a tool of God, sent by him to highlight the chinks and cracks which had appeared in the Christian religion? In which case, everyone was responsible for crimes against humanity and no one nation should congratulate itself on being tolerant as long as persecution was happening somewhere in the world.

"You know," continued Esther, " *'The only thing necessary for the triumph of evil is for good men to do nothing'* – this is an excerpt from a letter written by Edmund Burke and I think it is so very true!"

Chapter Ten

After Abi had gone home, Esther cleared away the tea cups and biscuits. While she did this, she pondered over the problem of the wooden doll. She should really be given back to the Finedon Church and yet, surprisingly, this did not feel right. It wasn't because she was heavily involved in the theft, either. It was because she felt the doll wanted something specific and by giving her back, the problem would not be solved. If only they could understand what the doll needed.

At home, Abi had finished off wrapping up Christmas presents. All she wanted to do now, was to be left in peace and to read some more of *Abigail's* journal, and so, after placing her presents under the Christmas tree, she hurried back upstairs to her room.

February 1692

Oh! I have started something I can no longer control! Betty and I have been sipping away at Tituba's medicine and our resultant fits and strange behaviour have caused mayhem within the parsonage. Uncle and Auntie have tried all manner of remedies to try and cure us. No doctor seems able to diagnose our complaint and the neighbours are beginning to whisper that we have been bewitched. Finally, one doctor, Doctor William Griggs, has confirmed that we have, indeed, been bewitched. Uncle Samuel has decided to try and use prayer to save our souls.

Tituba is on the very edge of insanity, I think. The news that we have been bewitched makes her even more erratic than usual. As soon as Uncle and Auntie were away from the parsonage, she listened to the advice of a neighbour, Mary Sibley, and concocted a witch-cake, made from rye meal and some of our urine and baked it in the fire and then fed it to one of the dogs. This, according to Goodwife Sibley, would cause the witch responsible for our sickness to reveal herself. Privately, I was pleased, having watched the ingredients being mixed together, that we didn't have to eat the cake!

What with secretly telling us stories of magic, keeping quiet about our dabbling with the Venus Glass, and now having baked the witch-cake charm, all within the boundaries of the parsonage, Tituba had a very guilty conscience. To protect ourselves, Betty and I started to blame Tituba for our worsening pains, by letting it be known that she had baked a witch-cake. Uncle was incensed and asked her if she was a witch. Tituba denied it, but she did admit to being taught by a witch in Barbados. The witch schooled her in methods of detecting and preventing magical harm. The witch-cake, Tituba pleaded, had been made to combat the harm being done to the girls, not to aid it. She never mentioned Goody Sibley's part in it.

Late one night, I was awakened by the arrival of two visitors to the parsonage. By creeping to the top of the stairs and listening, I was able to discern that they were Thomas Putnam and Doctor Griggs and they were talking to Uncle about our condition. Thomas Putnam and the Doctor were saying they did not believe in witchcraft but that most of the villagers did and so why not use the villagers' superstitions to their own advantage? This would allow Uncle to get rid of those villagers who were constantly against him and it would mean that Thomas could get his hands on some land. He would order his daughter, Anne, to start behaving in a similar fashion and the Doctor said he would order his niece, Elizabeth, to do the same. Thomas further said that he had it on good authority that Tituba often made a concoction as an aid for childbirth and he was pretty certain that I and Betty had been taking this concoction to bring on our fits. He also informed Uncle that it was Goody Sibley who had suggested making the witch-cake.

Uncle was incredulous and none too happy. We had managed to convince him that we were genuinely suffering and he did not like being made a fool of. He went on to say that it would all have been my idea and that his Betty would not have had the wit to dream up such tomfoolery. "What of Tituba?" asked the others. "Surely you can see her hand in all of this?" "Maybe," answered Uncle. There was silence for a while and I could hear someone, probably Uncle, pacing around the room in deliberation.

"Right!" he finally exclaimed. "If they want witches, they shall have them! But, first I must send Betty away to my sister. I do not want her tainted by it all. Abigail will continue to have her 'fits' and we will school and steer her, and Anne and Elizabeth, in the direction of who to accuse of bewitching them."

I held my breath. I had not bargained for anything like this! Behind me, in our shared bed, Betty stirred and I hurried back to bed, fearful that she might wake up and wonder what I was doing, listening at the top of the stairs. Tituba slept on as always. Nothing ever disturbed her, once she was asleep. I crawled between the covers and shivered. I was scared at what the coming months might bring.

Abi had to stop reading the journal as it was time for the evening meal and she was called down to assist with setting the table and other related chores. All through the meal she was preoccupied and as soon as she was able, she hurried back up to her room and carried on reading from where she had left off.

June 1692

After many weeks accusing those members of the village who were considered 'odd', and attending informal hearings, it was decided to have a Court of Oyer and Terminer so that the authorities could hear and decide whether these accusations carried any weight and to determine the best course of action. Betty had been duly sent away, and I was joined by Ann Putnam Jr; her mother, Ann Putnam; a cousin of Ann Jr called Mary Walcott and also by the Putnams' serving girl, Mercy Lewis. It was no coincidence that the other accusers were members of the same family.

Betty and I had been encouraged to accuse Tituba of being the one who had bewitched us. At first Tituba denied any wrongdoing, but then, she admitted to having been visited by a tall dark stranger and of having signed his book! I think Tituba was telling people what they wanted to hear in order to save herself. She also began accusing others of being witches.

Ann and I were constantly told, by Uncle Samuel and Thomas Putnam, which of the villagers to accuse of being witches. When we were in court, listening to the accused defend themselves, we were instructed to have our fits and to say we could see their familiars suckling on some part of the bodies of the accused. It all became quite vicious and I could see no way out of the mess. Although Uncle and Thomas took charge of the situation and were manipulating proceedings to suit their own ends, I feel that Uncle, nevertheless, blamed me for setting in motion all that happened in the village. Neighbour accused neighbour of all sorts of maleficence and there were even reports of witchcraft being uncovered in some of the other towns in New England. Accusations were spreading like a plague.

10 June 1692

On this day, poor Bridget Bishop's life ended, dangling from the end of a rope, the very first to be hanged. She had been accused by so many people of being a witch. Her accusers dredged up her misdemeanours from years ago, but it seemed their real objections to her centred around the fact that she dressed far too flamboyantly for a good Puritan woman and she had been married three times. I suspect her condemnation had more to do with spite and jealousy emanating from some of the women of the village, than from the likelihood of them seriously believing her to be a witch.

Bridget Bishop was the first of many, many more, who faced the same ending. When Betty and I had had our secret oomancy, I had had no idea of the trouble this would lead to. Our secret was exploited by those who see it as an opportunity to get rid of people they do not agree with or like, or as an opportunity to steal land.

My last testimony, if I can call it that, it being based on lies and manipulation, had been on the 3rd of June 1692. After that date, I became reluctant, obstinate even, to carry on. Uncle became quite angry with me until Thomas Putnam pointed out that they no longer needed me anyway. There were, by then, quite a few 'afflicted' girls and adults willing to accuse others of being witches. Thomas was also fearful that I might blurt out how they *had schooled Ann and myself in the art of being afflicted. With this worry in mind, it was decided it would be best if I was removed from Salem Village altogether. Uncle decided he would contact my family in England and send me to them at the earliest opportunity.*

Here the journal seemed to have reached the end of a chapter. Abi hadn't appreciated that it was written in two parts, with a gap of time between the end of one part and the start of *Abigail's* new life in England. Abi was hoping that the second part would reveal the link between the wooden doll and the church at Finedon.

Chapter Eleven

The 26th March 2020 was a date for historians. It was the first official lockdown due to COVID-19, where the entire country would grind to a halt and almost everyone had to stay at home. Abi, her brother and sister and all their friends were being homeschooled. No households were allowed to mix and people were only allowed out for essentials such as food and medical emergencies. Any exercise had to be taken close to home and only for an hour at a time. It was surreal... people felt as though they were living within a storyline for a film.

At first, for Abi, Ben and Nicola, it was fun. No school! However the novelty soon wore off. They missed seeing their friends and mingling with people other than their family.

Nicola had been enjoying a bout of popularity at school since her brush with online bullying. It seemed, suddenly, as though everyone wanted to be her friend. Lucy, on the other hand, seemed to have fallen from grace within their class. It had become common knowledge that she would be going to a private school in September and the rest of the pupils in her class seemed to think that she was too posh for the likes of them. The atmosphere towards Lucy was encouraged by Nicola. She saw it as a way of seeking revenge and revelled in Lucy's discomfort. This attitude of Nicola's was completely out of character for her and she found it hard to explain to herself, where these vengeful thoughts were coming from. Several times she wondered whether she had actually signed the book proffered to her in her weird dream... signed it and received popularity as a result. Could this have happened? Surely not! She was just letting her imagination run away with her.

Abi was reading *The Handmaid's Tale* by Margaret Atwood and, although the story was set in the modern day, possibly in the 1950s, she was struck by similarities between it and certain restrictions females found themselves living under in Salem at the time of the witch tragedy. She was also reminded of how easily the life you know and understand can change in a twinkling, as it had in *The Handmaid's Tale,* with a new set of laws and regulations implemented almost overnight. Abi drew parallels between this story and life for everyone at the moment, living under lockdown. Things had changed dramatically. For how long? She felt that the character, the narrator of the story, Offred, was very similar in her outlook to the character of *Abigail.* Both were living their lives under strict rules and obeying those rules, yet both were secretly critical of the regime under which they existed and both had recorded their versions of events, in the hope that someone, someday, would find their recordings and gain an insight into what was, essentially, first-hand accounts of the two girls' lives.

Her own essay on the Salem tragedy had been temporarily put on hold. It was looking like the play would not now be needed, anyway, as school had been suspended and people were not allowed to mix in large numbers. All the theatres were closed, so the chances of the Drama department putting on a production were nil. She had also lapsed in reading *Abigail's* journal, surprisingly. It was as though lockdown had brought about a certain kind of laziness. Yes she was keeping up with her school work, but she had a feeling of can't be bothered lying deep in her stomach. She had spoken to Michelle about it and Michelle too had had to admit that she found herself laying around and sighing a great deal. Michelle's dad was home a lot as there were no church services, although he had set up an online Sunday service on Zoom for his congregation to join in with if they wished. Susie and Josh were staying with Michelle's family during the lockdown. Josh hadn't had a recurrence of his sleep-walking and seemed none the wiser that he had even been sleep-walking.

Ben was missing doing Esther's gardening. Which greatly surprised him. He had to admit to himself that he found gardening therapeutic and he took out his various frustrations on the weeds. He liked Esther. She had a dry sense of humour and could be quite sarcastic, but in an amusing way. She would usually bake some delicious cake or biscuits to tempt him when it was his day to visit and garden and he was missing these sumptuous treats. When he thought of the trauma Jamie had put her through, and how that trauma and brought back painful memories of her childhood and the rise of the Nazis, he was glad he had made a stand, however late in the day, and had refused to go along with Jamie's intimidation of her.

Peg, the wooden doll, had also been quiet and none of them had been aware of her stomping around at night. It seemed as though everyone's life had been put on hold and Peg had picked up on this and was conserving her energy... but for what? Abi felt it was the calm before the storm.

Michelle, during one of hers and Abi's FaceTimes, had explained that she had had a conversation with her father about the wooden doll and he could remember, having been vicar to Warburton for many years and therefore mixing with other parishes, the story of the theft. He was amazed that the doll might have turned up, and if she was the same doll in question, had suggested that she ought to be returned to her rightful place. He had informed Michelle that he knew the current vicar of Finedon and that he was a 'most approachable fellow who used to be in a pop group' and had offered to have a word when their paths next crossed, or even to give him a ring on the phone, as long as Abi was on board with it. Michelle told Abi that she had not mentioned Esther and her friends' part in the theft, just that the doll had been found buried and that was all any of them knew.

Abi, on reflection, thought this would probably be a good plan. She had decided she would keep Esther out of the story and the secret of how the doll came to be buried in their back garden would have to remain a mystery. She ran this idea past Ben and Nicola and also past Ricky when he FaceTimed Abi. All were in agreement that the doll should be returned and that Esther's name should remain out of it altogether. The communication between Abi and Ricky had become quite routine and Abi was surprised to find that she had started to look forward to their FaceTimes. There was something between herself and Ricky, a little spark, which was gradually growing in energy and Abi found herself thinking about him more and more regularly.

Her feelings for Josh still ran deep, however, even though she knew it could never be and in fact, Josh never seemed to show much interest in her under normal circumstances and had definitely no conscious memory that they had kissed. Abi realised that her interest in Josh was of a physical nature in that she was attracted to him, but she did not 'know' him, whereas the relationship she was beginning to build with Ricky was something based on a mutual history of being at the same school, the same age, and knowing the same people. Ricky didn't make her heart bang when he entered a room that she was in, as it did whenever Josh appeared, but he did make her feel valued and it was obvious he was very much attracted to her.

Having decided to give the doll back, Abi and Michelle thought that it might be better if Michelle's dad could have a good look at it. This, under lockdown rules, wouldn't be easy to do, so it was arranged that Abi would leave Peg in the graveyard by the church when she went out for her hour's worth of exercise and then Michelle would pick the doll up when she then went out for her hour's exercise. This way, Michelle's dad would be able to describe the doll firsthand whenever he decided to contact the vicar of Finedon.

The weather during lockdown was lovely and warm. Summer had come early and it was such a pity that no one could go anywhere. People were spending time weeding and tidying and the village of Warburton had never had such well-manicured gardens!

One evening, Abi, having completed her homework, decided to take Peg and place her in the churchyard. She texted Michelle to let her know this was what she was going to do and Michelle answered with a thumb's up emoji.

It was just becoming dark when Abi entered the graveyard. There was no one else around and the place had a serene atmosphere. It was a lovely place, if such a location could ever be described as lovely, and was well tended by the parishioners and volunteers.

She had very mixed feelings about returning Peg to her rightful owner, as she had become very attached to her. She sometimes felt as though Peg had become a kind of talisman. She felt safe when the doll was near and found it almost unbelievable that Peg had once been used as a punishment at the Finedon school. Pushing all of these feelings to the background, Abi looked around for a suitable place to leave the doll.

As Abi began to walk around, she had the sensation of a cold hand slipping into her own hand which was down by her side. The sensation was so very lifelike that Abi found herself glancing to the side, expecting to find someone, Michelle perhaps, standing there. There was no one, however, yet the feeling of someone holding her hand persisted, and, to make matters stranger, she found she was being guided along the graveyard path and then across the grass towards an overgrown and forgotten area. If she tried to stop and change direction, whatever was guiding her would increase the pressure on her hand and tug her along. The whole thing was reminiscent of a book she had read a while ago, called *The Small Hand* by Susan Hill. The character in that story had also felt a small hand creep into his own whilst visiting an abandoned house. She had greatly enjoyed reading the book and was quite a fan of Susan Hill. However, as things were at the moment, Abi had to admit to herself that she was becoming a little scared by the sensation of being led along by an unseen force. It was one thing, curled up in the safety of bed, reading a ghost story and feeling deliciously scared yet safe, but quite another to be a part of this creepy scenario.

Abi's heart was hammering away in her rib cage. Through the trees she could see the lights of the vicarage shining through and she thought about calling out... maybe someone in the house would hear her? She tried but found that her throat had dried up and all she could manage was a squeak. The vicarage and its beckoning lights of salvation might as well have been a million miles away.

Finally, she was propelled to a very large weeping willow which lived in the farthest, darkest, most unkempt part of the cemetery. Bending over to avoid most of the long fronds of the willow, she passed under it. Here the grass was very long and it wound around her feet, nearly tripping her up. Eventually she came to a lone headstone which seemed very old in appearance and was sitting crooked in the soil, rather like a solitary tooth left in an old mouth. Here, the ghostly hand unclipped itself from her own, as though to say *here we are*.

Abi was uncertain what to do next. Why had she been brought to this place? She looked around in bewilderment and noted also that the night had finally arrived. Everywhere was in darkness and in this part of the graveyard, it seemed almost impenetrable.

After a short while, Abi's eyes adjusted slightly to the darkness and bending down, she investigated the gravestone. Any inscription on it had long since worn off and any mound of soil, which new graves have, was non-existent. The stone was simply wedged lopsidedly into the ground and was partially hidden by long grass and weeds. Who had been buried here, all alone, in this part of the graveyard, and why?

Suddenly, a hand appeared on the top of the stone and Abi drew in her breath sharply, hardly daring to look upwards beyond it.

"I'm getting so very tired of waiting," said a voice.

Abi finally looked up. Josh was there. His gaze seemed to cut right through her! At least it looked like Josh, sort of. In the dark, his features seemed more chiselled and although he was looking at her, he wasn't really seeing her. He seemed to be looking straight through her, as though she was not there.

"When can we finally be together? You told me it wouldn't be long now, that you have found a way," continued the 'Josh-like' figure.

Abi was uncertain as to whether she should answer. She had the feeling that he was not talking to her, but to someone she could not see. Someone standing behind her. She wanted to take a look but her head and neck felt as though they were fused together. The atmosphere around her seemed electrically charged, the same feeling as when a thunderstorm was brewing. Abi laid the wooden doll down in the long grass growing over the grave, then, her hands now free, she put them up to her eyes and covered them. If she couldn't see him, then he would not be there, whoever he was. She had decided he was not Josh, after all.

Gradually the charged atmosphere drifted away and she knew, without seeing, that she was alone. Slowly she took her hands away from her eyes. He was gone. Abi wasted no time. She decided this was a good place to leave the doll. She would explain where to Michelle. She hesitated, however, as she really did not want to part from Peg, but she knew she could not keep stolen property and that she had to be returned to her rightful place. Sadly, she left Peg behind, but thankfully she began her escape from the graveyard, running and almost tripping over on the uneven ground and accidentally running over old graves, as she hurriedly stumbled her way to the entrance.

Once at the gateway to the entrance of the graveyard, she found she could not undo the latch. Her fingers fumbled and fiddled with it, but it would not lift up to release the gate and allow her to escape. Abi kept glancing back, nervously, over her shoulder, checking whether something was coming up behind her. She knew she was being ridiculous, but she could not control the fear inside her. Finally, after she managed to break a couple of fingernails, the latch lifted upwards and the gate creaked open. Abi flew out of the graveyard and ran all the way home. She arrived breathless, appearing in the kitchen in a sudden flurry. Her mother looked up in a concerned fashion. "What on earth is the matter?" she asked, wiping her floury hands on a cloth.

"Nothing, really," replied Abi. "I've just dropped the wooden doll off at the graveyard for Michelle to pick up so that she can show it to her dad. I became a bit scared, that's all. Creepy places, graveyards."

Her mother nodded and carried on with her task of making the evening meal. Abi decided to go up to her room and gather her thoughts. Was it all in her imagination, or was there definitely a force which had led her to the lonely grave? She decided to FaceTime Michelle and tell her where the doll could be found. She wondered whether to share her experience of the strange happenings in the churchyard. On reflection, she decided not to relate the events at the moment and merely told Michelle where she could find the doll. If Michelle was surprised by the choice of hiding place, she didn't show it.

Abi was very preoccupied during dinner. She had finally got back her appetite for reading and she now wanted to carry on reading *Abigail's* journal. Abi needed to find out how the wooden doll had come to be at the village of Finedon. Hopefully all would be revealed in the next part of the journal.

Ely, Cambridgeshire, 1712

Today I have decided to carry on recording in my journal. I have had quite a break from writing in it. Years, in fact.

I remember I was very glad to get off the ship. I had discovered that I have not got 'sea legs' as I found myself being sick at the slightest of sea swells throughout the entire voyage. It was with a heartfelt pleasure that I disembarked the ship. This pleasure did not last, however, as being on dry land once again felt very strange as I had become used to walking the decks of the ship which would rise and dip underfoot. The land did not move but my legs still felt the need to prepare for any bobbing. The result was that I found it very difficult to remain standing and, curiously, I felt sick all over again. I was told this feeling would soon pass as my senses would eventually adjust to the new conditions.

After the ship I was on docked in Bristol, I was met by George Williams, a distant cousin on the side my father's family. This branch of the Cromwells, which had never changed their name from Williams to Cromwell, lived in Ely and had done since Oliver Cromwell had inherited a house from his uncle in 1636. The house in question came with a position as tax collector for the area and Oliver had carried out this task. Some members of the Williams family had followed him to Ely and had remained there ever since. So it was to Ely, and a new start in life, that we now travelled.

Life in Ely was pleasant enough, if a little quiet. Hard to imagine that it had once been at the heart of the Civil War and had provided men for Oliver's army. It was dominated by Ely Cathedral, or 'The Ship of the Fens', to give it its other nomenclature.

Being a Puritan family, George Williams and his wife, Anna, and daughters were not surprised that I could read and write and decided that my education should continue. To pay for my upkeep, I was given house chores to complete, in a similar way to my life in Salem Village. No mention of my life in the New World was ever approached. I do not know whether Uncle Samuel had informed them of the happenings in Salem Village, but I was never asked about my life prior to coming to live in Ely. Aunt Anna surveyed me with great suspicion and I was not allowed to have on show either my vase or the wooden doll. These *were to be kept from view and if they were not, I was told they would be destroyed.*

There was one person whom I idolised. I was to call her Aunt Frances, though our familial relationship was far too removed for her to be my aunt. She was one of the daughters of Oliver and she was a cousin of mine so many times removed. Nevertheless, the first time we met, we bonded. I like to think she saw something of herself in me. She would visit Ely, where she had spent most of her childhood before her family were elevated to the position of 'first family' and moved to live in Whitehall and Hampton Court, several times a year and would always seek me out. Aunt Anna was none too pleased, since Aunt Frances never seemed to pay her daughters the slightest notice.

Life carried on in this vein over the years and I grew from girl into woman. My future seemed to be set to continue in the same fashion until the day I would meet my maker. I was never introduced to society and there were no suitors. I was prepared for a very long and drawn-out descent into old age. Then, at the age of thirty-two years, my life changed. Aunt Frances had decided that I had been a servant to Uncle George and Aunt Anna long enough. I overheard her say that the events to which I had been unfairly involved in whilst living in Salem Village, had happened during my childhood and that I had more than paid my dues, living as nothing more than an unpaid servant. It was time, she had said, to allow me to spread my wings. A charity school had been founded in the village of Finedon in Northamptonshire, by Sir Gilbert Dolben, who was related to the Williams and Cromwells. The school was in need of someone to assist in the teaching of its pupils and Aunt Frances felt that I was a good candidate for such a position! Uncle George offered little resistance to my staying on as their servant, and so it was, with great pleasure, I embarked on a new chapter in my life. I packed up my few belongings and took the vase and the wooden doll with me to begin my life as a teacher in the village of Finedon.

So that was how the wooden doll had found its way to Finedon, thought Abi. At last she had found the proof that the stolen Finedon doll and Abigail's wooden doll were one and the same!

The rest of the journal was a lot sparser in terms of entries and Abi realised she was finally coming to the end of Abigail's diary. She glanced at the time. It was quite late, but nevertheless, she decided to carry on and reach the end.

The Charity School, Finedon, Northamptonshire 1713-1720

I am now writing my journal in the latter years of my life. It became increasingly difficult to keep up with my entries on a more regular basis. Being a teacher at the Charity

School took up so much of my time and I would fall into bed of a night so exhausted that any thought of writing in my journal was placed to the back of my mind. I knew I would return to it eventually and I hoped my memory would serve me well when I came to make my entries.

When I first arrived, I settled in well to my new surroundings. The Headmistress was very friendly and was interested in my wooden doll. She suggested that the doll should be on show and asked if she could be mounted above the front door, so that the girls would see her, carrying her Bible and scroll, and be reminded to always be pious as they went out into the world. I agreed, happy that at last Peg would not be spending more of her days living under my bed. So it came to pass that Peg's newfound position was above the front door in the entrance hallway.

At the beginning of my teaching, I found it very difficult to relate to the girls and they in turn seemed to sense my lack of experience as a teacher. An atmosphere of sullenness grew between us and instances of poor behaviour grew in number. I had no idea how to control my classes and feared I would be asked to leave by the Headmistress.

Then, one night, I was awakened by screaming. The girls' dormitories were on the same level as my rooms. I hastened to light a candle and carried it along the corridor to the room from which the noise emanated. Inside, I found Elizabeth, one of the worst culprits for the poor behaviour I have written about earlier. She was huddled up at the far *end of her bed, her body pressed against the wall, looking, for all the world, as though she wanted to disappear through it. The other three girls who shared the same dormitory with her, were, not surprisingly, all awake and seemingly at a loss as to what had so frightened Elizabeth.*

I sat down on the edge of her bed and tried to calm her down. I asked her what had frightened her. She replied that she had heard someone walking about and when she opened her eyes, my wooden doll was bending over her with such a ferocious expression across her face that she had become terrified. I suggested that maybe she had been dreaming and I gradually managed to soothe her and eventually everyone was able to return to sleep. Even so, I did go down to the hallway to check on Peg. I needn't have worried. She was there, hanging from the hook above the front door, looking her usual, serene self.

The next day there was a marked change in Elizabeth. She was very attentive in lessons and the poor behaviour she had once exhibited never arose again. Did I have Peg to thank for the improvement? I wasn't sure, but in the future, every time a girl stepped out of line, the same dream was always reported. The pupils became scared of Peg and, when it was time for the daily walk, would always hurry out through the front door, with eyes looking upward, fixed warily upon her, as she hung above them. Even the new pupils seemed to be scared of her and I guessed they had been told the stories of Peg's occasional nightly wanderings and retributions.

My vase, or Venus Glass, I kept in my room. I have never used the Glass as a simple vase before, having always to keep it hidden away with the wooden doll. I had decided I would use it to put some flowers in but, strangely, the flowers always died more or less straightaway. Moreover, anything which was put into it, such as hair combs or clips, was always found on the floor. I came to the conclusion that the Glass did not like anything inside it, except for that strange fog which would swirl around and I would fancy I could see faces hidden within it.

One night, I was aroused from sleep by a noise sounding like a door closing. I got up and peered out of my window, but I could see nothing of interest. My vase, on the other hand, had a thick fog in it once more, and as I looked at it, I fancied I could see one of my pupil's faces in it, staring out at me with a look of horror. I shook my head and went back to bed, convinced the girls' whisperings of supernatural happenings were beginning to unnerve me. I had had sharp words with the girl I had just supposedly seen in the vase earlier that day, during lessons. She seemed to have gained some sort of hierarchy over the other girls – not from popularity but more from maliciousness. I did not like her and the other girls knew it.

The following morning there was pandemonium. This girl had gone missing and after much searching, her body was found in the woods and she was without a stitch of clothing. It was a mystery as to the cause of her death. It was not long before the finger of suspicion was pointed at me. The Headmistress addressed me over the incident and it was apparent from her questions that she was aware of my background troubles in Salem Village. Of course, no evidence could be found that could be pinned to me, yet the Headmistress felt it would be best if my services at the Charity School were dispensed with. This would have been quite a catastrophe for me, as I would have had nowhere to live and although I had managed to save most of my earnings, I am not sure they would stretch to affording adequate living conditions. The year was 1720 and I had just turned forty years of age and the chances of getting another position were very slim, especially as my unfair reputation seemed to be following me around. However, my great friend and distant relation, known to me as Aunt Frances, whom I have written about already in this journal, had sadly passed away earlier in the year and, to my surprise, had left me, in her last Will and Testament, a cottage in the village of Warburton.

So my dismissal, whilst unfair and very upsetting, was not quite the catastrophe that it could have been. It seems to be my lot in life that I am to be unfairly used, blamed and punished for events which were out of my control. I feel I have been a pawn in the schemes of others all of my life and I am getting weary. I should have liked to find love and to have had children of my own, but alas, it was not to be.

I packed up most of my possessions. I say most, as the Headmistress wished me to leave the wooden doll behind. She liked the idea that the girls were scared of Peg and felt it gave her the upper hand and she wished to build on the legend which surrounded the doll. I balked at this at first. Peg was a reminder of my days living amongst the Native American peoples. It was a reminder of Takamunna , whom I had never forgotten, but then, as I thought about it, the doll had been made by Takamunna's father, Wamsutta , and it was the lizard which Takamunna had given me which kindled my thoughts of him, and I still had this. After much deliberation with myself, I finally said that I would leave the wooden doll behind and left to begin another new life in Warburton, once again leaving under a cloud of falsehoods.

1721 Warburton Village

At last I feel settled. The cottage belongs to me and no one can dispute this or take it away from me! It is a very curious feeling to be finally in control of your own life and destiny. Warburton is a very peaceful place to live. I keep myself to myself as I fear that the other inhabitants, if they get too close to me, may find out about my past and take against me. So, whilst I am not rude, neither do I allow much contact. I do attend the church services and stay around for a little small talk afterwards, although I feel the reverend of the church has heard about me. There is something in the expression in his eyes which alerts me to the fact that, yet again, my reputation goes before me. I do not think, however, that he has betrayed my past to the other parishioners... yet anyway.

I am not lonely, really, as I like my own company and am never short of things to do. I have a garden at the back of the cottage which I have cultivated and there is a wood which I enjoy walking in and it has a path which is a shortcut to the church.

I have been in correspondence with Betty Parris, or Baron as she is now, my cousin from Salem Village, who was sent away when the witch trials began. She sent a letter to Uncle George in Ely, having been given the address from Uncle Samual, and Aunt Frances delivered it to me, at the Charity School, the last time I was to see her alive. It was comforting to hear from Betty, as I had often thought about her over the years. Betty married Benjamin Baron in 1710 and they have four children, Thomas, Elizabeth, Catherine and Susanna. Whilst I am delighted that Betty has found love, happiness and has four children, I am nevertheless envious of her. She tells me that her father, my Uncle Samuel, passed away on the 27th February 1720 and that just before his death, he finally gave in and let Betty have the address to which I had moved to after Salem Village. Apparently she had been asking for this address for many years. The family had left Salem Village, soon after the end of the trials and Betty now lives in Concord, Massachusetts. Another piece of information Betty divulged was that our friend Ann Putnam had made a confession and revoked her accusations of witchcraft! I was greatly surprised by this.

Betty also went on to tell me, in her letter, that a mysterious, well-dressed, gentleman of a rather dark complexion had arrived at her house and had been asking about me. He said his name was Jonathon Adams. He wanted to know where he could find me. He told Betty that he and I used to go fishing together and that he had made a promise to find me. Betty explained to the gentleman that she had only just found my address and was about to write to me and hoped the letter would find me after all these years. She told the man that she would ask me if I wished to see him and that he would have to wait for my answer to arrive. He had replied that he would stay in the area and find employment in Concord to pay his way.

I felt sure that the man was Takamunna and lost no time in replying to Betty's letter, making sure I included my latest address in that reply and telling her that I would be happy to see him again. Would he be able to travel across the Atlantic though? In any event, hopefully waiting for him to turn up, gave a lift to my days, although I fretted about the colour of my hair. It was beginning to turn grey and had lost some of the golden hue which Takamunna had so loved.

Time went on as before, with me filling the days tending to my vegetable patch and attending church. The reverend appeared to become more hostile towards me, just in little ways. His eyes were cold and unsmiling when he greeted me and after the service, where he would shake most people by the hand and thank them for attending, he never extended the welcoming hand of friendship to me. I began to feel that the other parishioners were taking note and a subtle withdrawal of deference towards me was taking place. It may have been in my imagination, of course, but I sincerely felt that it was not.

I also had developed a problem with my hearing. I constantly could hear whispering, as though someone was behind me, whispering into my ear. I could not make out any words and so I began to believe that my hearing was at fault in some way. Yet, the same whispering noise also seemed to come from my vase, especially when it had that curious fog with the half-hidden faces stirred up in it. I was suffering from nightmares too. The faces of the women I had accused of witchcraft often visited my dreams at night. I would wake up in a cold sweat, having relived those terrible times through my sleep. One such night, the faces of the women were replaced by that of a man, dressed in black and wearing a tall, black hat. He ordered me to sign the book and said that if I did, then all the bad dreams would go away. I must have tossed and turned in my bed, because when I finally awoke, the sheets were all in disarray. I remember I glanced at the vase, which was sitting on the windowsill, and I was sure I could see the remains of the face of the same man, with the same tall black hat, being swallowed up in the swirl of mist within the vase.

Tituba had talked of just the same man having visited her. Betty and I had assumed she was lying. Was I simply just rehashing her description of him, in my dreams? Or had she been telling the truth and this character did exist?

One thing was certain. The vase, or Venus Glass, which had been used by Jane Throckmorton and then by Betty and myself, for our oomancies, now seemed threatening. It seemed to want something. I have never had these feelings about it in all the years I have owned it and I struggle to think what has changed, for me to feel this way about it? Am I losing my mind, or is there really something of the supernatural surrounding this vase?

1722 Warburton Village,

Finally Takamunna has arrived! I needn't have worried about the change in my aged appearance, as our renewed friendship continued where it had been suddenly cut off all those years ago. Takamunna, or Jonathon, as he is now known, is quite the refined gentleman although the spirit of the Native American peoples still resides within him. His mother, Angeni, who I have written about earlier in my journal, had been, like myself, taken hostage by the natives, but, unlike me, had never been 'rescued'. However, Takamunna – I shall carry on calling him by this name when we are alone in my cottage – explained that soon after I left their camp, there had been an attack by the settlers which had almost wiped out their little community. His father, Wamsutta, had been killed, along with many, many others. Takamunna's mother, Angeni, had, as a consequence of this attack, been reunited with her proper family and she and Takamunna had been taken in by them and Takamunna had received an education and been turned into a gentleman. He had trained as a doctor and was quite well thought of in the medical world. He had been given the Christian name of Jonathon, after his grandfather, and the family name was Adams. Hence his new identity. All was not quite such plain sailing, however. His dark complexion was testament to his mixed parentage, and not everyone gave him the respect he deserved. In some circles he was called a half-breed and treated with contempt.

Takamunna's staying with me in my cottage gave rise to raised eyebrows amongst the residents of Warburton. Takamunna attended church along with me on Sundays and I could tell that the parishioners did not know whatever to make of our situation! I loved this and felt a little bit of the young and rebellious Abigail returning. The reverend was the worst of them all with his haughty superior attitude and I classed him in the same league as the Reverend Parris. Both were as vain and as untouched by God's hand as each other. I despise them both, even though one is now dead.

Takamunna set up his doctor's practice in the cottage and soon had a steady stream of patients attending his surgery. He charged far less than other doctors in the area and to most people, this was enough for them to repress any feelings of prejudice they might have had towards him.

Life carried on in this happy fashion. We were as man and wife and I was so happy to have at last found love even if I was now too old, it would seem, to have children.

Then, a darkness began to form on our horizon. Takamunna developed a nagging cough and would be taken ill for a number of days with a temperature, before becoming well again, except for the tickling cough. I was reminded of the story Aunt Frances had told me about her first husband, Robert Rich. He too had developed a cough and it eventually was the cause of his early death. Takamunna gradually became very ill and it was obvious to us both that he was not going to survive. I nursed him day and night, despite him warning me not to breath in the same air as him. He urged me to wear a face cover whilst attending him. My best efforts were to no avail and Takamunna passed away. I was devastated. It seemed I was still being punished.

The reverend would not allow Takamunna to have a Christian funeral, or to be buried in the churchyard. "I'm not having that heathen lying amongst proper God-fearing souls" were his exact words. I fixed him with a stare, my eyes burning into the very substance of his skin, hoping he was feeling my blazing anger and hatred. So I buried Takamunna myself, in the woods at the edge of the cottage garden. I paid some young men to dig a grave and in it I placed Takamunna's body. I found a large, flattish stone to place as a headstone and so mark the spot where he lays. At least he would be near to me as I continued to live out my days in the cottage.

With his passing, there was a return of the whispering and the vase seemed to become, once again, threatening and I was being visited in my dreams by the poor women I *had helped to condemn as witches. I have bemoaned the prejudice which Takamunna had faced yet it was largely prejudice which had sent those women to their deaths in Salem Village, that and greed, of course. I had been a party to it and I hated myself for it. In my defence, I had been a mere child and had been used as a pawn, but still I felt enormous guilt.*

One night, just a day or so after Takamunna had died and I had been to see the reverend, I was visited again, in my dreams, by the tall man in the black hat. He shook the book in my face and said if I signed it, then Takamunna would be buried in the churchyard and the reverend would have an unfortunate accident. I could feel my resolve slipping. It would be nice to see the reverend suffer. He could suffer on behalf of Reverend Parris too. I began to dream of suitable tortures for them both and woke up sweating, my nightdress soaking wet. I quickly got out of bed, knelt down beside it, pressed my hands together and prayed for forgiveness.

The reverend remained safe and well and poor Takamunna was buried in the woods, so I presume that I managed not to sign the book after all.... if such a book exists.

I have come to the decision that the reason the vase seems to be gaining in power over me is because the wooden doll is no longer around to protect me. I remembered when Wamsutta gave me the wooden doll he had carved for me. He had told me then that she had been charged with looking after me, in place of the parents I had lost.

The doll was my guardian and I had left her at the Finedon school. The vase was evil and I think she had kept its malevolence at bay... and now she was not around...

There were no more entries and Abi put the journal down. She was worried about *Abigail's* last revelation... *The wooden doll was no longer around to protect her...* and Abi had just left Peg in the graveyard. Could it be that it was not the doll which was malevolent, but the vase? Abi thought back to all the curious incidents which had happened... The whispering, the fog inside the vase, the fact that it didn't like anything to be put inside it.

I need to get the doll back, thought Abi and wondered whether to ring Michelle. Surely she now had the doll safe and sound at the vicarage? She picked up her phone with the intention of ringing her friend, but then realised what time it was. Michelle would be sound asleep and it would be unfair for Abi to disturb her. Tomorrow would do. She was about to put her phone down again when she noticed that Michelle had tried to contact her several times and there was even a voicemail. Abi had had her phone on silent all night as she didn't want to be interrupted whilst reading the journal to the end. Dialling up her voicemail, she listened to the message which Michelle had left. It wasn't good news. Apparently, Michelle had gone to the graveyard to pick up the doll as instructed, only to find that she wasn't there. Michelle had explained exactly where she had gone to get the doll and Abi agreed to herself that her friend had gone to the right place. So where was the doll?

On a whim, Abi crept down the stairs and into the lounge, where the vase was currently on display. It had a thick fog inside it and there was whispering all around. Abi stared, transfixed by it. Faces seemed to appear in the thickness of the swirl. They came and went as though the vase was showing off all the souls it had collected through the ages. Finally the swirling slowed down and seemed to freeze on one face alone. It was the face of her sister, Nicola.

Chapter Twelve

"Is everything okay, Abi?" asked Nicola. Abi whirled around. Nicola was standing behind her. Abi glanced back at the vase. Her sister's face was no longer visible. Had it merely been a reflection?

"Yes, I couldn't sleep and came down for a glass of water," replied Abi, knowing that this was a lie. "I thought I heard a noise from in here and just popped in to check on things," she continued.

Nicola nodded. "Me too. I mean, I came down for a glass of water, too."

After getting drinks of water from the kitchen, the girls walked together back upstairs to their bedrooms, saying goodnight on the landing.

Once back in her room, Abi still couldn't sleep. She opened her bedroom window to let in some fresh air. The night was very mild, following the heat of the day, and the fine weather looked set to continue. She was worried. *Abigail* had stated in her journal that she felt the doll was her guardian and that it had been protecting her from whatever spirit was inside the vase. She had left the doll at the Finedon school and had then noticed an increase in activity from the vase. Abi had left the doll in the churchyard and now, it seemed, she was missing. What was this to mean for Abi and her family, isolated due to lockdown and alone with a malevolent force? There were no more entries in *Abigail's* journal, so Abi could not even find out how she had dealt with any further supernatural episodes emanating from the vase.

She decided to FaceTime Ricky. Yes, it was very late, but he was the only other person who could read the journal and she needed his insight and thoughts on the latest turn of events described by *Abigail.*

Ricky seemed to take an age to answer her call, but eventually, after using the call back button to reconnect after she had been cut off, her screen suddenly filled with the image of a tousled and sleepy Ricky.

"Abi, what the… do you know what time it is?" he asked, sitting up in bed. He was wearing Spiderman pyjamas.

Abi let out a little laugh. "Spiderman! How cool do you look!" she exclaimed in a teasing voice.

Ricky responded by putting up two fingers and then pulled his bed covers up under his chin. "I wasn't expecting company tonight," he said, grinning. "Anyway, to what do I owe the pleasure?"

Abi wasted no time in bringing Ricky up to speed with the whole of the latest news on both the missing wooden doll and what *Abigail* had written regarding the guardianship of the wooden doll.

"Do you know what… I have always had the feeling that the wooden doll has been looking for something," explained Ricky. "I think she is looking for *Abigail* and has been all these years. Think about it… a spell was put on her charging her to look after the motherless *Abigail,* and having been left at Finedon, she went on the walkabout looking for her charge. I think she has always had *Abigail's* best interests at heart, which is why she tried to sort out the misbehaving girls."

"What about the fact that Ben and Nick, as well as me, have heard her walking about at night here?" asked Abi.

"She is still looking for *Abigail* but also I think she has somehow confused you with her. You share the same name and, it would seem, are descendants of *Abigail,*" answered Ricky.

Abi thought about this for a moment before continuing. "We can only be of the same family, not descendants, Ricky, because *Abigail* didn't have any children, so would the doll still want to protect me? And why just me? Ben and Nicola are related too!"

Ricky shrugged. "I really don't know enough about this kind of stuff… does anybody? I'm kinda making this up as I go along, but it does seem to make some sort of sense, don't you think?

"It's possible," conceded Abi. "I'll have a look on the internet and see if I can find anything which might shed some light on our problem… You know, reports of similar happenings, that sort of thing."

"Good idea," answered Ricky, scratching his head and yawning.

"Sorry to have disturbed you, Ricky. I hope you can get back to sleep."

"It's all good, Abi. Glad you felt you could contact me," replied Ricky, winking and disconnecting.

It was four o'clock in the morning and Abi had not had any sleep, and it seemed, was unlikely to get any now. Her mind was buzzing and it would be pointless to try to settle down. Instead she went on Google, asking a question about supernatural reports involving wooden dolls.

The first item to come up seemed, on the face of it, to have all the right 'noise' surrounding it. It concerned a married couple who devoted their lives to helping those people who were bothered by paranormal problems. Americans, Ed and Lorraine Warren, were known as Paranormal Investigators and had had dealings with a wooden doll known as Annabelle. However, when Abi read further she found that it was the film adaptation which made the doll wooden, when in fact, the true story surrounded a Raggedy Ann doll supposedly possessed by the spirit of a young girl who was known as Annabelle, hence the name of the doll. All this had taken place in 1968. There was a lot of scepticism over whether Ed and Lorraine were genuine, noted Abi. She decided that the story didn't really have that many similarities with her wooden doll after all, as Peg had had a spell put on her and was not possessed by any spirits as such. What was of interest, though, was a paragraph she read that reported on an interview with Ed Warren, where he stated that objects were not possessed by spirits but were used as a tool by demonic forces which wanted to possess the owners of the objects. Immediately, Abi thought of the vase. She knew the vase had been used as a Venus Glass in an oomancy twice before. Once by Jane Throckmorton (according to *Abigail*) and once by *Abigail* and *Betty*. Had it been used more than this? It was obviously very old and had been in the Throckmorton family for a long time. Had it been a tool for some evil force all this time? Was this what had made Jane Throckmorton turn on her neighbour, Alice Samuel? Was it the vase which had played a part in the Salem Witch tragedy? It seemed the more Abi delved, the more questions she wanted answers to and realised that she would probably never know for sure what some of the answers might be. She then remembered an earlier idea she had had, where she had thought the vase was similar to the story of the lamp which contained a genie. She turned her attention to researching the history of genies. Walt Disney's *Aladdin* couldn't be further from the truth! The genie, or jinn, dated back centuries, pre-Islam and pre-Christian and seemed to originate in Mesopotamia, modern-day Iraq, and the demon known as Pazuzu was associated with them, Abi was amazed to read. She carried on researching and then read something which was extremely unsettling.

"In the year 2000, teachers at an all-girls school in Jeddah, Saudi Arabia, began having seizures and fits and although doctors attributed this incident to mass hysteria, many believed that jinn inhabited the school."

Was it possible that it wasn't the special brew made from ergot, the fungus which grows on rye, that had caused *Abigail's* and the other girls' fits? Was it just a coincidence that the fits came on just as they had begun to drink the concoction? Maybe, thought Abi, it was the vase and its resident spirit which had been behind the Salem Witch Crisis. Perhaps *Abigail* and *Betty* dabbling with the oomancy had attracted the evil eye which had brought forth the atmosphere to give false accusations...

Chapter Thirteen

Muriel was sitting in her room in the care home, reflecting. A memory was nagging away in the depths of her head. It was something to do with Jean, and Muriel felt it was something she needed to remember and pass on to Esther. She chewed at her thumb nail, a habit of hers which she had had since childhood. *The vase*, she thought to herself. *It has something to do with the vase*. She studied a similar vase currently sitting on her windowsill in the hope that it would fire her imagination and therefore her memory. She had remembered that Jean's vase did not seem to like anything being put into it and that it sometimes had a curious smoky fog swirling around in it... but there was something else. Something Jean had once said, after the doll, vase and book had been buried. What was it?

Then she remembered!

"Gemma!" She called out to a passing nursing assistant as she walked past Muriel's room. Gemma doubled back and popped her head around Muriel's open door.

'Yes?" Gemma answered, her voice muffled inside her mask. Her plastic apron rustled as she moved to flick her fringe away from her eyes with her gloved hand. She was thankful she had managed to get hold of some personal protection for herself. Masks and aprons were in very short supply.

"Would it be possible to give my friend, Esther, a time when she can visit me here in the home, please?"

"I'm afraid not, Muriel. We have a strict Covid restriction in place which means no visitors. You can ring her if you like… do you have a mobile phone?"

"Yes," replied Muriel as she picked up the phone which had been resting on the little coffee table close to where she was sitting. She peered at it doubtfully. It had been a little while since she had used it and she struggled to remember how she could make a call on it.

Gemma took pity and offered to set up the call so that all Muriel had to do was select the call button when she was ready to do so. After first wiping down the phone with an antibacterial wipe, Gemma scrolled down through Muriel's contacts and found the name she was looking for. Handing the phone back to Muriel, she instructed her as to which on screen button to tap on when Muriel wished to place the call and then left to carry on her duties.

Muriel tapped the call button and waited for Esther to pick up her phone. It seemed to take a little while, but eventually Esther answered.

"Hello, Esther speaking."

"Esther? It's Muriel. Can you hear me? I'll speak loudly so you can catch what I'm saying."

"There's no need to yell in my ear, Muriel! I can hear you perfectly well if you speak at the normal level," replied Esther. "It's nice to hear from you, by the way. How are you?"

"Bored!" answered Muriel with a disgruntled tone to her voice. "It's this blessed virus. We have to stay in our rooms most of the time and we aren't allowed to have any visitors, at least not inside. We can chat to family members through the window, but it's not the same. You can't have a good old chin wag when you have to screech your business at each other across a windowsill."

"I can imagine it's quite difficult. I'm largely on my own too. I have created a bubble with the new family who live in Jean's cottage, so I do have some company at least, but it's no way to have to live, is it? How long is this going to go on for? It will be ages before they manage to create a vaccine to combat the virus. Anyway, is this a courtesy call, or is there a specific reason for which you have rung me?"

"Yes. It's about the vase. I've remembered something Jean once told me. She reckoned that it was the vase which was the real problem and that the doll had been misunderstood all of these years."

"What on earth made her think that? The only thing she could ever talk about was the doll! The vase never came into it – not to my knowledge anyway," answered Esther.

"Think back to the night we buried the doll, Esther. You weren't actually there when we dug the hole and lowered the trunk into the ground. Afterwards, you had the idea that all three items, the doll, the vase and the book, were all buried at the same time, which isn't strictly true," replied Muriel.

"Okay... Go on – what did happen, then?"

"It was just the doll at first. Jean liked the vase, and she wanted to read the book. After a while, however, the vase began to get on her nerves. It made a noise like someone whispering and Jean was of the opinion that she could see faces in that peculiar fog which sometimes appeared in it. She became scared of it and also some of the things she read about in the book made her feel very uncomfortable and so the burial site was opened up and the vase and book were deposited in the trunk and the hole was once again filled in. Afterwards, Jean said that the book and the doll and the vase were linked and that the book had been written by someone called *Abigail Williams*, who had become infamous, apparently, although I've never heard of her. Jean said the book explained that the doll was some sort of guardian," explained Muriel.

"Yes the book was written by *Abigail*," replied Esther. "Young Abi has been filling me in. I'm not sure whether she has finished reading the journal yet though and there is some talk of giving the doll back to the vicar of Finedon in due course."

"Has the girl mentioned anything about the vase, though? Has she said whether she thinks it's odd or sinister?" asked Muriel.

"Not really. She did once tell her mum that she didn't want it in her bedroom, so maybe she has noticed something," said Esther. "Tell me, did burying the vase work? Was that an end to Jean hearing whispering and such like?"

"I'm not completely sure that it did. Jean had relief from hearing the doll once the doll had been placed underground, but I do believe she could still hear whispering even after the vase was buried. Don't let Abi give the doll back... not yet anyway. The doll is keeping them safe from harm, if what Jean said is to be believed," replied Muriel, with an insisting edge creeping into her voice.

"Okay Muriel. I'll see what I can do but it isn't easy being sociable at the moment... Not with this virus hanging around..."

At the vicarage, Michelle had decided to ask her father if he knew, or had any information about whose was the solitary grave lurking under the willow tree in the graveyard.

Reverend Peter Tooley regarded his daughter over the top of his glasses, which he typically wore half way down his nose. "I'm afraid I have no idea, Michelle," he replied. "Why do you ask?"

"Abi stumbled across it the other day and asked me if I knew," replied Michelle, not wanting to admit that the wooden doll was left there and now she was missing. Her dad might think that Abi had decided to keep the doll after all and he probably would not approve.

"We can have a look at the old church records if you like. I know this church has a graveyard plot map. Does the gravestone still have a readable inscription on it?"

Michelle shrugged her shoulders. "I haven't really looked. I suppose it can't have or else Abi wouldn't have asked who the grave belonged to," she answered.

"Hmm, let's go to my study and look at the grave map. I've recently made a fresh copy of it so we don't have to keep handling the old one. You can point to the grave you are talking about and I can cross-reference it and find a name," said Peter.

Father and daughter went to the study. It was a cosy room with a desk and chair, PC and screen and two comfortable-looking armchairs sitting either side of a large hearth. Reverend Tooley held his parishioner appointments and Parochial Council meetings in this room. Tall bookcases, the shelves of which were bowing under the weight of all they had to support, surrounded the walls.

Peter went over to one of the bookcases and selected a file. From it he took out a folded sheet of paper. Taking it over to his desk, he unfolded the paper and smoothed it out. Shoving his glasses further up his nose, he then beckoned to Michelle to join him at the desk.

Michelle gazed at the paper. It was a map of the graveyard, marking out the graves, each with a number written on them.

"There have been no new burials in this churchyard since 1950. Instead the graveyard on the edge of the village has been used as an overflow since that year," said Peter, explaining to his daughter. Michelle nodded, she already understood this. Graveyards fill up and new land has to be consecrated in order to receive new occupants.

"As you correctly point out, the headstones of graves become so worn that they are rendered unreadable," Peter continued. "This is why it is essential to keep good records of just who has been laid to rest in the graveyard. It has become a very popular pastime to try to find one's ancestors and church records can give lots of answers."

Father and daughter worked together. Peter was able to cross reference the grave plot number with the list of names he had written on a different paper.

"According to this, and I have taken every care to reproduce the information carefully from the very old papers, the grave belongs to a woman known as Abigail Williams, who died in May 1724," said Peter, whipping off his glasses and looking speculatively at Michelle. "Rather a coincidence, isn't it, that Abi should be interested in a grave that just happens to have the same name as herself? Care to enlighten me?"

Michelle was silent for a moment. The story really wasn't hers to divulge, yet she didn't wish to upset her dad by being secretive. "I need to talk to Abi first, Dad, before I tell you anything. Please understand that it's her business and if she is agreeable, I will tell you everything that has been going on."

"All right. As long as you give me your word that I shouldn't be worrying about you? I need to know that you are not caught up in something which is causing you to have sleepless nights," said Peter, an authoritative edge creeping into his voice.

Michelle gave her word and got up to leave the study. On her way out, she stopped and said "Thanks, Dad," and quietly closed the door.

Reverend Tooley stared reflectively at this door for a while. He wondered whether there was any more information he could find out about *Abigail Williams*. Was she the same character of *The Crucible* fame, he wondered. Surely not. He turned to his records of births, marriages and deaths and found that in 1723, *Abigail* had given birth to a daughter, whom she had christened Frances, and the baby's surname was that of her mother's, *Williams*. So the father was unknown and not present then. He checked in the marriage register but could find no mention of any marriage between *Miss Williams* and A Another. He looked in the deaths register, and found *Abigail Williams*, but noted that she was buried alone and there was no record of the death of Frances Williams, so the baby had apparently lived and must have moved away. Of course, with her mother dead, someone would have had to take responsibility for the orphaned Frances. He wondered what had become of her.

Ben entered the kitchen. He had been working out in the garage with his dad, helping him to put shelves up and had been sent in to get two glasses of water. As Ben turned on the tap, he thought he could hear a noise coming from the lounge. He knew his mum and sisters were upstairs carrying out various tasks, so it couldn't be them. He turned off the tap and went to investigate.

Once in the lounge, he was able to pinpoint where the sound was coming from. Over on the windowsill the vase was once again full of thick mist and a sound of whispering came from it. Ben remembered that Abi had said the vase seemed to whisper, but he had never witnessed this first hand before. He also remembered Jamie saying he thought the vase was weird when he had come across it one day when he had been visiting Ben.

Ben went over to the vase and watched it. Faces seemed to appear in the mist. They came and went as though they were on a carousel. Round and round they went, every face different until the carousel stopped and froze on one of them. Ben instantly recognised it. Jamie! Ben shot backwards. What on earth! He stared at the vase until the face within disintegrated, like the shape within a cloud which only lasts for a very short while. The vase was now just full of a swirling mist and no more faces appeared. The whispering continued, though, and Ben found he was slowly approaching the vase. He had an urge to place his ear over the top of the rim. He was slowly bending towards the vase, his head to one side, ready to listen to the whispering.

"Ben!" yelled Abi. "Get away from the vase!"

Once again Ben shot backwards. "What's the matter? I wasn't doing any harm!" he grumbled.

"I've told you that the vase is strange. You put your ear to it to listen to the whispering and it seems as though it wants to suck you into it," explained Abi.

Ben thought about having seen Jamie's face in the vase. Had he put his ear to it?

"I saw Jamie's face in the vase," he replied. "Do you think that's the reason he seems to have changed so much?"

"I honestly don't know, Ben. All I know is that it tried to draw me into it but I managed, somehow to escape. I think it was the wooden doll which saved me."

They both watched the vase for a bit and then their dad could be heard calling Ben from the kitchen door.

"Oh! I'm supposed to be getting us a drink!" said Ben, and he scurried off to fulfil his errand.

Abi went back upstairs to finish off some school work. The vase had lost its audience. The mist within it carried on swirling and a wisp of smoke wafted upwards and floated above its receptacle.

Michelle had contacted Abi and they had arranged to meet up in the graveyard for a socially distanced chat. Michelle wanted to ask Abi whether she would mind if Michelle told her dad the whole story and also to tell her that the mysterious grave belonged to *Abigail Williams* and that she could tell her the year that *Abigail* had died! She further mentioned that *Abigail* had given birth to a daughter, who was called Frances.

Abi was very interested to know this information and mentally noted that *Abigail's* death happened not long after the final entry in her journal.

"*Abigail* must have been expecting then by the time of her last journal entry! She mustn't have known though, as she makes no mention of this. She must have died giving birth perhaps, or shortly afterwards, from complications. She was quite a mature age to be having her first child."

"Possibly," answered Michelle.

Abi was surprised, however, that Michelle wished to tell her father everything.

"Why, Michelle?"

"Well, he queried the fact that you were interested in a grave which turned out to have the same name as yourself. He said it seemed to be a bit of a coincidence and was there anything I wanted to tell him. I said that the story wasn't mine to tell, but I think maybe he could help us to sort it all out, perhaps," she answered, half expecting Abi to firmly say it was none of her father's business.

"Hmm," said Abi, frowning while she considered what her friend had just said. She did feel as if they were in the middle of something of which they were fast losing control. Maybe it wouldn't be so bad to have an adult's perspective on this and given the, sort of spiritual, otherworld nature of things, a vicar might just be the type of person to have a receptive ear. Having read all of *Abigail's* journal, she now knew that Takamunna was buried in the woods under the strangely shaped stone and, from the 'sightings' she had witnessed in the woods and in the graveyard, that *Abigail's* and his souls wished to be buried together and Abi wanted to fulfil this need for them. To do this, she would need the help of someone who was used to dealing with death and burials.

"Okay... Yes, I think it would be a good idea for your dad to be brought in on this," she finally answered.

Michelle let out a sigh of relief. "Great! Let's set up a Zoom conference then, between our two households and Ricky. I think Ricky should be part of this as he can back you up over being able to read the journal."

Abi nodded her agreement.

Ricky was puzzled. How was it that only he and Abi could read the journal? He wouldn't have given it any thought if it had been just Abi who could read it... but why could he read it too? A suspicion was forming in his mind. He rang one of his cousins whom he knew had researched their family tree and told her the name he was looking for and asked her to check whether anyone in their family line had had that name. His cousin agreed to scroll through her information and said she would get back to him as soon as possible.

Ricky waited impatiently for his cousin to call back. Meanwhile, Michelle contacted him to arrange a time when he could join in with her and her dad and Abi and her brother and sister in a Zoom call.

"Your dad?" asked Ricky, raising his eyebrows.

Michelle nodded. "Abi is going to bring him into the fold, so to speak, and tell him everything. We think we need help to sort all of it out," she said, doing her best to explain.

Ricky didn't appear convinced. "I'm not sure he will believe us! It is a bit of a tall story! I'm not sure I would believe us if I wasn't involved!"

"He's quite open minded and often talks about the possible existence of the supernatural – I suppose a vicar has to be. If you think about it, even religious stories take some believing. The very act of worshiping someone unseen and whose existence cannot be proven takes a lot of faith," replied Michelle.

"Well, as you say, it's Abi's story to tell. I can be free any time so just text me when your dad is available."

Just after he had finished talking to Michelle, his cousin rang him back.

"Ricky," she said when he answered. "You're right! There is an Abigail Williams in our family tree! A long way back – born in 1680. She's our grandmother so many times removed and she had a daughter called Frances who in turn had two daughters, Elizabeth and Sarah, and the family line carries on in this vein right down to the current day!"

Ricky listened as his cousin gave him some more information and then thanked her for getting back to him so promptly.

His suspicion had been confirmed. The reason he could read the journal was because he was a descendant of

Abigail Williams, as was Abi. This meant he and Abi were very distantly related.

Chapter Fourteen

There was silence all around as Michelle's dad digested all the information he had been given over the conference call. Part of him wondered whether he was having his leg pulled, yet he trusted his daughter implicitly and knew she would not be a party to wasting his time. If the story was true, and not a figment of their imaginations, then the vase with its sinister occupant was going to be a real problem. A source of evil which was slowly wafting into their lives and preparing to do damage.

"Hmm," he said, placing his hands together in a prayer-like fashion. "I'd like to test this theory of yours. I'll have some of the people I use to dig graves and ask them to dig in the area of this funny stone which is in the woods. If they find a skeleton buried there, then I shall believe what I'm being told... not that I'm calling you liars, you understand, but it is quite a fantastic tale and I'm sorry, but I do need some proof. Of course, if bones are found, then the police and other authorities will have to be involved, if only to prove the burial site isn't fairly recent and to rule out the site as a crime scene. Does this course of action appeal to you?"

Everyone nodded in agreement. Abi was relieved that the vicar hadn't laughed outright at them and told them to run along and find something useful to do.

"Thank you, sir," she said. "How soon will you be able to get this done?"

"I'll get on it right away. The gravediggers can wear masks and largely keep their distance from each other. It is their work after all and so we won't be breaking any lockdown rules," replied the vicar.

A few days later, Michelle was able to confirm to Abi that bones had indeed been found at the spot in the woods, by the rounded stone. Michelle said her dad was now finally convinced that everything they had told him seemed to be true. As had been warned by the vicar, the burial site was now a temporary scene of crime whilst the necessary authorities carried out their search of the area.

"There are people from the forensic department and policemen, Abi! It looks like a scene from *Line of Duty* and, unfortunately, it's caught the interest of a couple of journalists. Dad said when it's proven that the burial site is an old one of an insignificant person, then hopefully the journalists will lose interest," said Michelle excitedly.

Abi was amazed that something had been found at the site. She had been pretty certain that the weird happenings she had experienced over the last few months were real, but, even so, a little voice in her mind had kept whispering that maybe she was getting carried away and merely imagining things.

"So what happens now?" she enquired.

"Well, Dad says that we have to wait for all the tests to prove that this is not a recent burial and that no crime has been committed, and then he's mentioned re-burying the remains along with *Abigail's* in her grave under the willow tree," replied Michelle.

"Really! He doesn't mind doing that? I'm sure that's what *Abigail* and Takamunna want! Oh I can hardly wait. Will we be able to attend the burial?" asked Abi, excitedly.

"Not sure," replied Michelle. "Don't get too excited, there may be a long wait and then the burial might have to be done without anyone attending."

"Well, I intend to be there, even if I have to hide behind a tree to watch," said Abi, a determined expression descending over her face.

That night, for Abi, turned out to be a very scary one. She was woken up in the early hours of the morning. All was very dark except for a curious light, coming from behind her curtains, and glowing on her windowsill.

Not again, she thought. *Whatever can it be? The vase is downstairs, so it can't be that.*

She got out of bed and pulled the curtains back. The vase was sitting on the windowsill! *How can this be?* she thought. Maybe Mum, or one of the others had returned it to her room? She couldn't be sure, though. Which meant that perhaps the vase had somehow put itself back on her windowsill. A shiver of fear ran around her body. What did the vase want? What was it capable of? Had it really turned neighbour against neighbour in Salem? Did it seek out a person's weakness in their personality and provide temptations which ultimately built on that weakness until that person became a prisoner of the vase? Abi thought about all of the faces she had seen hiding within the depths of the smoke in the vase. The smoke was strange in itself as it did not give the impression of having been born from fire. It was more like a mist or fog. As she watched the vase, not knowing what steps to take to do something about it, the mist began to slowly rise up out of the container. Quickly, Abi got out her iPad and selected a file to which she had saved some research on the Jinn. She had read something about an amulet, in the form of a ring, which had been given to King Solomon, which had given him the ultimate power over all Jinn, both good and evil. Apparently, King Solomon had had dealings with a churail (a big demon) who, when threatened with being burned had asked for mercy and had given King Solomon the amulet as protection to be worn, against itself. The amulet was known as the Seal of Solomon.

As Abi read through her research, she kept glancing nervously at the ever-thickening cloud which was gathering above the vase. Whatever it was, it was coming out! The demon had given King Solomon its name as part of the deal to save itself. Abi had also read that demons did not like to have their name used against them. She carried on reading, her heart in her mouth, searching for a reference to the name which the churail was known by. Her eyes sliced over line after line as she attempted to speed read and the quickness of her eyeballs, swivelling from side to side began to make her feel sick. At last she found the name.

"Himatah!" she shouted at the vase. Instantly the fog began to descend back into the vase! The mist appeared to dry up, the curious light disappeared and the vase was back to normal. Abi couldn't believe her eyes! Had she finally banished the demon from inside? Or was it merely waiting, biding its time, until it could regather? Her gut feeling was that the demon was still resident in the vase.

Abi was going to have to think of a way to silence the demon permanently.

After what seemed an age, the relevant authorities were content that the burial site was of no interest to them and released the bones for a burial. No one was interested from an historical or archaeological point of view either. It wasn't as if Takamunna was famous, as in the case of King Richard III, who had finally been found buried beneath a car park in Leicester. Reverend Tooley was free to carry out the re-burial at a time convenient to him.

Ricky had mentioned to Abi that it seemed they were related, if the family tree was traced far enough back in time. Abi was quick to make the connection between this piece of information and the fact that Ricky could read the journal.

"But if that is the case," she said in a reflective tone, "why can't my dad or Ben and Nicola also read it? They too are related to *Abigail*, yet they all see the journal as a soggy mess."

The screen image of Ricky shrugged his shoulders. "I have no idea, Abi. Like I said before, none of this makes any sense and we are trying to understand it as we go along. Maybe there are no set rules. The reason you and I can read the journal is... just because."

Abi nodded. "We'll probably never understand exactly what is going on. I think we ought to bury the book, the vase and the wooden doll all together along with *Takamunna and Abigail*. Then I think we will be able to draw a line under all of this."

"Having just told me that you think the vase is the object of all the evil, and that whatever is in it is trying to get out, do you think a simple burial will contain it?" asked Ricky. "Besides," he continued, "the wooden doll is missing, don't forget. Be a bit hard to bury her when you no longer know where she is!"

"True," answered Abi, agreeing. "I'm going to research a bit more to see what's out there to keep an evil spirit at bay!"

Ricky chuckled. "I'd like to see your search history... I bet it's got lots of really weird stuff on it!"

True to her word, Abi carried on researching around the information of King Solomon and his powers. She found some interesting ideas and ordered some items which she hoped would assist their needs, when it came to it. Her main worry now was in hoping the products she had ordered would arrive in time to protect them all from harm.

Chapter Fifteen

Reverend Tooley checked his diary to see when it would be convenient to have the reburial ceremony. He was interested to see that he had a window of opportunity the following afternoon. Picking up his mobile, he rang one of his gravediggers to confirm that he and his accomplice could be present at the graveside tomorrow.

"I'm sorry, Reverend Tooley, but Kevin has come down with a dose of Covid and is having to self-isolate. I'm okay though, as I haven't seen him for a while and I've tested negative anyway, but I can't dig the grave out on my own," said the gravedigger, apologetically.

"Oh dear! I hope Kevin isn't having too bad a time of it," replied Reverend Tooley. "I can ask my daughter's boyfriend to help out. Josh is pretty useful with a spade. Would you mind working with him?"

"That should be fine. I can do the bulk of the work. I just need help with some of the digging. I don't mind working with a novice, if it gets a job out of the way."

"Excellent, Paul. I'll see you tomorrow then at around three pm."

That evening in the Williams household, Abi had decided to tell her parents about *Abigail*, the wooden doll and the vase. She invited her brother and sister to join her and together they explained everything to Robert and Mary.

"If it wasn't for the fact that Michelle's dad is now involved, I would be telling you to get a grip and stop letting your imaginations run away with you!" exclaimed Robert.

"I must admit that the vase and its curious fog and how anything that is put in it seems to die straightaway has made me wonder," said Mary, after silently digesting the information her children had just told them.

"And you say that Reverend Tooley is going to perform a reburial?" asked Robert.

Abi nodded. Suddenly a look of understanding passed across Robert's face. "This explains the strange conversation I had with an undertaker just the other day! A Mr Holywell rang me and said he had been given my name by Reverend Tooley. Mr Holywell said he urgently needed a carpenter, which of course is what I am, to make some repairs to a coffin. Apparently this coffin had never been used as it had been damaged when it had accidentally been dropped and had been sitting at the undertaker's premises, gathering dust, ever since. It needed a new panel and Reverend Tooley wanted to use it to help someone in his parish who could not afford to pay for a proper funeral. I asked if this was allowed and Mr Holywell said of course it was and that he was glad the coffin was finally going to be used. I understand now! This coffin is to be used for the reburial!"

"Have you made the repair, Dad?" asked Ben.

"Oh yes! I went to the undertaker's place and worked on the new panel."

Abi was impressed with Reverend Tooley's initiative. It seemed that there would be no real expense towards the cost of the reburial.

"So, this is all happening tomorrow?" asked Mary.

Abi nodded. "There's no need for you and Dad to be there. Reverend Tooley said he would prefer it if it was just me, Ben, Nicola, Ricky, Michelle and we'd like to invite Esther, if she's up for it. We have to be careful of numbers because of Covid."

Abi's parents nodded. In truth neither really wanted to be involved anyway. They both felt it was a little on the macabre side.

"I'm still not convinced about all of this mumbo jumbo," said Robert.

The scene in the graveyard, the following day, was a strange one. *Abigail's* grave, under the weeping willow, had been reopened and a deep, oblong hole dug out and the resulting soil piled high to one side, ready to be shovelled back once Takamunna's coffin had been lowered into its depths. Some of 'The Gang' and Esther were waiting, keeping their distance from each other and wearing masks. Reverend Tooley had yet to arrive as did Abi. Ben was on his way across the graveyard, carrying the vase, the bulbous base of it already swirling thick with fog. The two gravediggers, of which Josh was one, were standing leaning on their spades, sharing a conversation about the football teams they each followed.

"Where's Abi? asked Michelle of Nicola.

"She said she'll be along as soon as possible. She's waiting for an Amazon delivery apparently. It's due any moment according to tracking. She's asked that we don't start until she arrives," replied Nicola.

"Well, I hope she hurries up. My dad will be here soon and he won't want any hold-ups. What's so important about this delivery that it can't wait?"

"It's got something to do with all of this," answered Nicola, using her finger to draw an imaginary circle around the graveyard. "Something to protect us," she continued with a shrug of her shoulders.

The girls were standing a little distance away from each other and so had to speak quite loudly in order to make themselves heard and also to overcome the muffling caused by their masks. As they were talking, Ben arrived and put the vase down. The fog, by now, had crept up the neck of the vase.

"By the way," said Nicola to Michelle. "What did you make of Josh kissing Abi like that?"

Michelle's eyes were wide over the top of her mask. "She told you about that? Wow!"

"What's this?" asked Ricky. His eyes were blazing over the top of his mask. Unknown to him, the fog in the vase had begun to escape and had swirled its way, like mystical tendrils, around his legs and upwards.

"Um... Josh kissed Abi... but he doesn't know as he was sleepwalking at the time," said Nicola.

Uh oh, thought Michelle.

"Sleepwalking, my arse!" exclaimed Ricky. He was extremely jealous. He glared across at the unsuspecting Josh. He felt his legs carry him across to where Josh was standing.

Josh looked at him and gave a wink. "All right mate? Something I can do for you?" he asked, in all innocence.

The wink added fuel to Ricky's mental fire. "You jerk!" he shouted, shoving Josh backwards so that the spade he was nonchalantly leaning on fell to the ground. Ricky picked it up and began brandishing it. The fog had followed him and was thickening around him, giving him the appearance of a vengeful genie.

"What's your problem?" asked Josh, squaring up to Ricky. They were both breathing heavily and the area of the face masks surrounding their mouths pulsated, at once being sucked in and then blown out. They were like two bulls snorting at each other.

"Oi, stop it, young man! There's no need for this sort of behaviour. Put the spade down!" yelled Esther.

The rest of the group had been struck dumb and were standing rooted to the ground. Esther glanced at them and thought, *Where's Reverend Tooley when you need him?*

Ricky swung the spade back over his shoulder, adopting the stance of a cricket batsman about to strike a six. Just before he let fly with the spade, the wooden doll appeared from nowhere, and stood between the two boys.

"Jeez! Where did you come from?" asked a surprised Ricky. He lost his balance and fell over, dropping the spade at the same time. The fog left him and moved on to claim Josh, who looked set to pummel Ricky into the ground. The doll woodenly twirled around and fixed Josh with her inscrutable gaze.

"Himatah!" yelled Abi. She had just arrived and had taken in the trouble with one glance. The fog began to recede back into the vase and the sinister atmosphere evaporated from the graveyard. The aggressive expressions on the faces of the two boys also disappeared, leaving both boys looking puzzled and wondering what had just gone on.

Abi approached everyone, slipping a pendant over their heads, one at a time. These were the articles which Amazon had just delivered. Michelle held hers up to inspect it. It was made of metal and was a small ornate hand with a six-pointed star in the middle of the hand, on the palm, rather like the Star of David.

"What's this?" she asked.

"Well, the hand is a hamsa and the star is the Seal of Solomon and it represents a powerful amulet against evil," answered Abi.

"I'm not sure my dad will be too pleased at us wearing this kind of tat!" exclaimed Michelle.

"Oh, it's not tat," said Reverend Tooley, who had just arrived and was ignorant of the scene which had just taken place. "The hamsa is a symbol which predates all religions and in fact has been adopted, certainly by the three main religions, Christianity, Judaism and Islam. For Muslims it is the Hand of Fatima, in the Jewish religion it is the Hand of Miriam and in Christianity it is the Hand of Mary. Abi is right, it is a powerful protector and more powerful still when combined with the Seal of Solomon."

Reverend Tooley had not arrived alone. There was another gentleman, also a vicar, accompanying him and everyone looked at him with interest.

"This is the vicar of Finedon, by the way. I've been telling him your story and of course, he is very interested to learn that the wooden doll has been found."

"Oh wow!" exclaimed Ricky, who was still brushing himself down and smoothing his hair back into place. "Didn't you used to be in a pop group?

"Yes that's right, I was," replied the vicar..

"I'm in a band called *The Fen Tigers*," Ricky said proudly. The vicar smiled and nodded and was about to reply when his attention was taken by his sighting of the wooden doll.

"Oh my," he said, going over and picking her up. "I've only seen photos of her and never seen her for real. She's much larger than I expected."

"We are hoping to bury her in the same grave as *Abigail and Takamunna*," explained Abi.

"Ah, yes," said the vicar, and he looked uncomfortable. "I've had a talk with my parishioners and I'm afraid they are adamant that they would like the doll to be returned to St Mary's. I'm sorry, but there isn't anything I can do except to carry out their wishes."

Abi looked crestfallen and Ricky would have liked to put his arm around her and, but for the social distancing, he would have done too. Instead he had to console himself by saying, "Never mind, Abi, I think her work is done anyway."

"I suppose so," said Abi reluctantly.

"Right," said Reverend Tooley. "Time to perform this reburial, I think. So, Abi, are you still going to place the vase and the journal in the grave?"

Abi thought for a moment. She decided that she wanted to keep the journal after all, so that just left the vase to be buried. She pulled out of her bag another package which she unwrapped. Inside was a cloth with the Seal of Solomon emblazoned on it. She quickly picked up the vase and wrapped it up in the cloth. "This, I hope, will keep whatever is living in the vase quiet for ever more."

The group, managing to stay distanced, gathered around the burial site. Takamunna's coffin entered first and then Abi lowered the vase into the grave and Reverend Tooley said a few prayers. After that, it was the job of the gravediggers to fill in the hole. Reverend Tooley thought it might be nice if *Abigail's* gravestone could be cleaned up and Takamunna's name added at some point in the future and he said he would ask the congregation to see if they were willing to contribute towards the cost.

Ricky and Josh nodded to each other. Josh was still in the dark about his sleepwalking and the kiss and the others in the group decided to keep it that way. Ricky was surprised by how violent he had felt as he had never experienced this emotion before. Was it the mysterious fog which had played with his emotions? In a way, he hoped so, and he hoped that Abi believed that, too. He didn't want her to think he had a violent streak. Their relationship was on hold at the moment, due to the virus, but when things were back to normal, he was certain that Abi would agree to a date.

The vicar of Finedon spirited the wooden doll away and Abi was sorry to see her go and it was with some sadness that the Williams family made their way home with Esther, as she was invited to tea as the family were part of her bubble.

All was fine for several months. No more noise of someone walking about, no more fog or whispering. Everything felt back to normal.

In the graveyard, buried deep, the vase was full of thick fog. It swirled around and images of faces flickered in the usual carousel. Round and round they went until it stopped and focused on one face. One member of 'The Gang'. For now the fog was contained but it would only be a matter of time before that member was moved to dig the vase back up. The protective cloth which Abi had used to wrap it up would soon rot and then the power within the vase just had to wait for the person held within its grasp to play their part.

In St Mary's Church, Finedon, the wooden doll had been welcomed with much joy. Her disappearance in 1980 had finally been solved, although no one knew who had stolen her, and she was back where she belonged. Her return had caused quite a stir within the community and with the local newspaper and TV station.

Peg wasn't happy to be back in the church. She was honour-bound to look after her charge and she knew that she was still needed.

So, it was with surprise and sadness that, one morning, when the new vicar of Finedon entered St Mary's Church, it was noted that the wooden doll was missing… again.